ONE SNOWY NIGHT

AMANDA GRANGE

© Amanda Grange 2002
This edition © Amanda Grange 2012

The moral right of the author has been asserted

No part of this publication may be reproduced, stored in a retrieval system, or transmitted in any form or by any means without the prior permission in writing of the publisher. Nor be otherwise circulated in any form of binding or cover other than that in which it is published and without a similar condition including this condition being imposed on the subsequent purchaser.

This book is a work of fiction. The characters and incidents are either fictitious or are used fictitiously. Any resemblance to any real person or incident is entirely coincidental and not intended by the author.

First published in hardback by Robert Hale Ltd. under the title of Rebecca's Refusal

Praise for Amanda Grange
"Absolutely fascinating" – *Historical Novel Society*
"Hits the Regency language and tone on the head" – *Library Journal*
"Lots of fun" – *Woman* magazine
"Rich atmospheric details" – *Publishers' Weekly*
"Affectionate" – *Washington Post*
"Sure to delight Austen fans" – *Cheshire Life*

cover image - www.timelinedesign.co.uk

By Amanda Grange
(Some books previously issued under different titles. Original titles in brackets.)

Regency Romances
A Most Unusual Governess
The Earl Next Door (Anything But A Gentleman)
The Six-Month Marriage
One Snowy Night (Rebecca's Refusal)
The Silverton Scandal
One Night at the Abbey (Carisbrooke Abbey)
Lord Deverill's Secret
Harstairs House
Castle of Secrets (Stormcrow Castle)

Edwardian Romances
That Would Be A Fairy Tale (Marriage at the Manor)
Titanic Affair
(Set on board the ill-fated liner, *Titanic)*

Jane Austen Fiction
Mr Darcy's Diary
Mr Knightley's Diary
Captain Wentworth's Diary
Edmund Bertram's Diary
Colonel Brandon's Diary
Henry Tilney's Diary
Mr Darcy, Vampyre
Pride and Pyramids (with Jacqueline Webb)
Dear Mr Darcy

For more information please visit her website at
www.amandagrange.com

Chapter One

Ah, well! At least nothing else can go wrong today, thought Miss Rebecca Foster as she made her way up the stairs of the coaching inn, a lighted candle in her hand. *And thank goodness for that!*

The freezing cold day in the January of 1814 had been full of trials and tribulations. In the morning Rebecca's companion, Miss Biddulph, had been taken ill and Rebecca, whose journey was urgent, had had to leave her in the care of a local apothecary. Then Rebecca's coach had become stuck in a snow drift, delaying her so badly that she had been forced to seek a room at an inn, instead of travelling on to her aunt and uncle's house in London.

She had taken the last room, and as it was very cold she had told her maid to leave the unpacking until a fire had been lit and the room had warmed through. Then she had retired to the parlour for something to eat, and now she was looking forward to returning to a cheery glow and settling down for the night.

She reached the top of the stairs and turned along the corridor, glad of the flickering candle which lit her way. She reached her room and opened the door, and then stood stock still. For there, standing not six feet away from her, was a strange gentleman - in the act of undressing!

Her first thought, as she took in the unexpected apparition, was that she must have returned to the wrong room, but a glance around the apartment told her otherwise. It was the same small chamber she had taken earlier that evening, with its dark red paper on the walls and its thick rug covering the floor. The only difference was that the fire was now aglow.

Her second thought was that, if she had not mistaken the room, then the gentleman must have done so. She was about to point this out to him when he turned around and her courage faltered, for she became uncomfortably aware that he looked very like a lion. He had glowing eyes, strongly contoured features and a thick mane of tawny hair. His lithe and muscular body, clad in breeches and a half-buttoned shirt, continued the impression of a jungle animal.

Realising she must speak before her courage failed her, she said, 'I do not know what you are doing here but I would be obliged, sir, if you would immediately leave the room.'

'Now why would I do that?' he asked, looking at her as though she were his next meal.

'Because you have no right to be here. This is my room,' she said.

'It doesn't seem that way to me,' he returned.

Thinking that he had arrived to find the inn was full, but that he had somehow stumbled into an empty room and decided to keep it, she said, 'I took it earlier this evening, the room is mine, and as I am not about to give it up, I would be obliged if you would be on your way.'

He looked at her levelly.

'Would you indeed? I am sorry to disappoint you, but I have no intention of leaving.'

'Neither have I,' returned Rebecca, stepping firmly inside the door.

'No?' His eyes took on a predatory look and his mouth curved as he removed his cravat and threw it on the bed. 'I am very pleased to hear it. Then by all means, stay!'

She was about to take him at his word and sit on the bed when she had the alarming feeling that he would regard it as an invitation. There was something very particular about the way his eyes were travelling across her ebony locks, her porcelain-white skin and her naturally red lips, before drifting down over her delightful body. It made her feel very weak in the knees.

Knowing that she must bring the matter to a hasty conclusion, she said, 'I only left the room to take supper downstairs, I cannot think how you came to be here, but I must ask you to go.'

'A good try.'

His mouth curved sardonically in evident disbelief and, as if to stake his claim, he continued, provocatively, to undress.

Rebecca swallowed and was momentarily nonplussed, but she had no fancy to spend the night sharing a bed with her maid. Reminding herself that she came from a long line of determined people who had risen from poverty to prosperity by persevering against the odds, she said, 'If you do not believe me you may ask the innkeeper.'

But he casually swept her challenge aside.

'I haven't the slightest interest in asking the innkeeper,' he returned. 'The room is mine and I intend to use it.'

'Do you mean to tell me that you have paid for it?'

'I have indeed, and paid handsomely, this being the last room at the inn.'

'Then it seems there has been some double dealing,' said Rebecca, realising that the innkeeper, seeking to make as much money as possible out of the calamitous weather conditions, had double let the room. 'In a situation such as this a gentleman would customarily defer to a lady —'

'Would he? You have been in a similar situation before, then?' he asked wickedly.

'No, not precisely, but —'

Her mouth dried as he pulled his shirt out of his breeches and her next words refused to come out. He had undone all the buttons, which ran from neck to chest, and he was lifting his arms as if he was going to remove it altogether. She had a sudden urge to flee – until she realized that that must be his intention, and so she stiffened her resolve and continued.

' . . . but . . . ' she said, stopping again in mid-sentence as he pulled his shirt over his head, his muscles rippling as he did so. She swallowed. 'In that case,' she said again, trying not to look at his tanned and muscular chest, 'I am sure you would not want to deprive me of somewhere to sleep tonight.'

'No. You're right. I wouldn't.'

She breathed a sigh of relief as she realized he was going to give way after all. And not a moment too soon, for she was not sure how much longer she could have persevered. She had a strong character, but she was beginning to discover that the gentleman in front of her had one that was as at least as strong as her own.

Her relief was short lived, however, for his eyes caressed her again, more intimately than before. Then he threw his shirt on the bed and said outrageously, 'You're welcome to share.'

To her annoyance she felt herself blush, but she was determined to have one last try.

'Am I to understand that you refuse to leave the room?'

'Yes, you are,' he said with a mocking smile.

She was not a woman who liked to admit defeat, but she knew when she was beaten. The only course left to her was to retreat with as much dignity as possible.

Saying haughtily, 'Then it seems that I must be the one to leave,' she turned and walked out of the room.

Once in the corridor she berated the innkeeper soundly under her breath. She would have berated him soundly to his face as well if she could have found him, but he had made himself scarce. The innkeeper's wife, too, was nowhere to be found, and so she was left with no alternative but to retire to her maid's attic room.

'Oh, Miss, I was just coming,' said the girl.

She lifted a pile of nightclothes out of the trunk that was open by the bed and headed for the door.

'I am afraid there has been a muddle, Susan,' said Rebecca. 'My room has been given to someone else. We will have to share.'

She sank onto the bed, annoyed, for she did not like to be bested. Her one consolation was that she would be leaving the inn first thing in the morning and so she would never have to see the leonine man again.

Her thoughts were not shared by the man in question, who would have been very happy to see her again. He had met many spirited wenches in his time, and many meek young ladies, but her combination of spirit and gentility was new to him. And that blend of dark hair, ruby red lips and porcelain skin was very attractive.

He should have been annoyed with her for trying to steal his room, and for inventing such a plausible story in order to drive him out, but instead he admired her for it. He had always been a man to take what he wanted, and it was not often he met with a kindred spirit. What a pity she had not accepted his offer to share his bed!

He indulged himself with memories of her delicate face and curvaceous figure, before he suddenly frowned. It was strange, but somehow she reminded him of someone. But then he shook his head. No. She could not remind him of anyone. He knew no one with such striking colouring. And yet there had been something. Something about her determined manner and the shape of her chin . . .

No. It was gone. He could not catch it.

Oh, well, she had provided him with an interesting interlude in his journey down to London, but it was probably a good thing she had not accepted his offer of sharing his bed, because it was serious business that had brought him back to England, and he had no time for distractions.

However charming those distractions might be.

Thank goodness! thought Rebecca as her coach rolled out of the inn yard the following morning. Her journey so far had been fraught with difficulties and she was relieved to be on her way. Her coach joined the London road and she turned her attention to the beautiful scene outside the window. Although the weather was icy the sky was a brilliant blue, and the snow was a lovely sight.

She snuggled down beneath her travelling rug, settled her booted feet more comfortably on her stone hot water bottle and gave herself up to an enjoyment of the view.

Towns and villages passed by, until at last, just before lunch, she entered the capital, and from there it was but a short journey to her aunt and uncle's house in Sloane Street.

As the coach finally rolled to a halt she gave a smile as she saw how pretty the house looked under its winter coating. The small-paned windows were covered in frost, the window sills were piled high with snow, and icicles hung from the portico.

Shaking out her travelling cloak she climbed out of the carriage and stretched her stiff legs before going up the stone steps to the front door.

'Welcome back, Miss Foster,' said Canning, the butler, as he opened the door.

'Thank you, Canning.' She smiled, pleased to see his familiar face.

At that moment her aunt, having heard the coach, hurried into the hall to greet her.

Mrs Hetty Marsden was an elegant woman of some five-and-thirty years of age. She was dressed in a fashionable high-waisted gown of dark green silk, with a Cashmere shawl thrown over her shoulders to keep out the winter chill. She greeted Rebecca warmly, taking her hands and then embracing her.

'Rebecca! We thought you would never arrive! But let's not stand here talking in the hall. You must be frozen. Come in!'

Rebecca returned her aunt's hug, then accompanied her into the drawing-room. She looked round the familiar room with pleasure. It was elegantly proportioned, and was furnished with taste and style. Hepplewhite chairs and damasked sofas were arranged in satisfying groups; small tables inlaid with rosewood and satinwood were dotted conveniently about; and a collection of paintings depicting classical scenes adorned the walls. A large marble fireplace dominated the far end of the room, and a welcome fire burned in the grate.

With stiff fingers Rebecca removed her bonnet and cloak as her aunt rang for tea.

'You look tired,' said Hetty, having ordered some refreshment. She took in Rebecca with an affectionate eye.

'I am,' Rebecca admitted. 'The journey was long and difficult. I am pleased to be finally here.'

'When you did not arrive last night I couldn't help being worried,' said Hetty. She sat down beside Rebecca on the gold-damasked sofa. 'But your Uncle Charles was far more sensible. He said you must have been delayed by the weather.'

'The weather was dreadful,' agreed Rebecca. 'The roads were slippery and in several places the coachmen had to dig a way through the snow. But the worst part was when Biddy was taken ill. In the end, she was too poorly to continue. I had to leave her behind, in the care of a local apothecary.'

'Oh, poor Miss Biddulph. Still, you did the right thing. The journey would only have made her worse. A draughty coach is no place for someone who is ill. She is to join us here when she is better, I hope?'

'Yes. She will travel on by the mail.'

'Quite right,' said Hetty approvingly. 'If she is recovering from an ague she will not want to be too long on the road, and the mail coach is always quick.'

The door opened and tea was brought in. Revived by a hot drink and a piece of seed cake, Rebecca told her aunt about the rest of her journey.

'Where did you stay last night?' asked Hetty, pouring Rebecca a second cup of tea. 'It was a good hostelry, I hope? The food tolerable, and the sheets properly aired?'

'I stayed at *The Queen's Head*,' said Rebecca, sipping her tea.

'*The Queen's Head*?' Her aunt frowned. 'I don't know it. How was your room?'

A sudden memory of her room, complete with partially-dressed gentleman, flashed into Rebecca's mind. She almost choked on her tea. Quickly she put down the cup.

'Unfortunately the inn was so full I had to spend the night in the attic with Susan.'

She mentioned nothing of her encounter with the leonine gentleman. She was uncomfortably aware that she had not behaved in the most ladylike of fashions. She should have fainted or had a fit of the vapours, or at the very least left the room at once, instead of bandying words with a partially-clad gentleman. If her aunt ever heard about it, she would be sure to disapprove.

'How awful!' said Hetty. 'Well, never mind, you are here now, and that is what matters. And you have still managed to arrive in time for the reading of your grandfather's will.'

The reading of the will was the reason for Rebecca's journey to London. It was to take place that afternoon.

'That is why I pressed on with the journey, instead of staying with Biddy,' said Rebecca. 'I knew it would be difficult and frustrating for Charles to have to rearrange the reading, and besides, I'm sure you must be wanting to know how things have been left.'

'It will certainly make life easier,' remarked Hetty. 'Particularly as the will was missing for so long. It was only by the greatest good fortune it was ever found.'

'It was typical of Grandfather to keep it himself, instead of entrusting it to his lawyers,' said Rebecca. '"They're rogues, Becky," he used to say to me,' she remembered with a smile. '"Lawyers . . . bankers . . . they're all the same. Rogues and rascals, Becky - every man Jack of 'em. Don't have anything to do with 'em until you must."'

'Typical indeed!' agreed Hetty. 'And it was just as typical of him not tell anyone where he had put it, once he had had it drawn up. He did not expect to die so soon. In fact, I do not think he expected to die at all. He expected to live for ever.'

Jebediah Marsden - Rebecca's grandfather and her uncle Charles's father - had died some time before, but his will had only recently been found, tucked away in a copy of Shakespeare's plays.

'It's hard to believe he was the son of a cobbler,' said Rebecca, looking round the room. She took in the elegant furnishings, the expensive paintings and the superb marble fireplace. She thought of her dearly beloved grandfather. He had taken advantage of the opportunities that had come with the new manufacturing industries, and he had made a fortune. 'Our family has come a long way.'

Hetty nodded. 'Jeb was an extraordinary man. But now, I mustn't tire you. You will need all your energy for this afternoon.' She stood up. 'I will show you to your room. I'm sure you'd like to refresh yourself after your journey.'

Rebecca, too, stood up and followed Hetty out of the drawing-room.

'We will be taking luncheon in an hour,' said Hetty. She led Rebecca upstairs, to the pretty guest room that had been made ready for her. 'And then we will be setting out for the lawyer's office.'

'And now I will leave you,' said Hetty. 'Remember, lunch is in an hour.'

Hetty left the room and Rebecca went over to the washstand, where a jug of hot water was set next to a pretty porcelain bowl. As she washed her hands, she laughed to herself. She already knew some of the terms of her grandfather's will - "I'm going to set the cat amongst the pigeons, Becky, lass," he'd said with a twinkle in his eye, as he'd told her about them – and she knew what a fuss they were going to cause!

Chapter Two

After partaking of an excellent luncheon, Rebecca changed out of her carriage dress and into a rose-coloured kerseymere gown, in preparation for her visit to the lawyer's office. The cheerful colour, worn so soon after her grandfather's death, would have been shocking to the ton, but Rebecca did not care a jot. Her grandfather had never cared for custom, and he had decreed there should be no period of mourning for him. "Tomfoolery for jackanapes!" he'd called it, betraying his lack of Society roots. "I've no time for people rigging themselves out like crows every time someone turns up their toes. You wear something cheerful, lass, that's how I like to see you."

She smiled as she thought of it. She missed him. But consoling herself with the fact that he'd had a long and happy life, she recalled her thoughts to the present.

Regarding herself in the cheval glass to check that she was tidy she adjusted the fine woollen folds of her gown. They draped themselves elegantly around her shoulders before falling from soft gathers beneath her breast into a long, slender skirt. She smoothed the long sleeves and tweaked the lace at the bodice and cuffs, and then sat down in front of the dressing-table so that Susan could arrange her hair. The maid brushed her ebony locks before pulling them into a neat and glossy chignon and then teasing out a row of ringlets round her face.

Well, she was ready.

'My dear, you look lovely,' said Hetty as she reached the bottom of the stairs. 'Now, we had better go. We will be meeting Charles at the lawyer's office. He is longing to see you again.'

'As I am longing to see him.'

The two ladies fastened their cloaks, settled their bonnets on their heads and pulled on their gloves.

'This snow!' exclaimed Hetty as they went out of the house. 'It looks lovely, but it does make things difficult.' She turned to the coachman, resplendent in his livery, who was sitting on the box. 'You will go carefully, won't you?' she asked anxiously. 'Mr Marsden is very concerned about his horses.'

The coachman assured her that he would take care and the two ladies stepped into the carriage.

'It's just such a pity Joshua could not be here,' said Hetty as the carriage pulled away. 'Charles wrote to him as soon as Jebediah died, but he has had no reply.'

Joshua Kelling was Jebediah's godson. Rebecca had never met him, for they lived in different parts of the country, but her grandfather had spoken highly of him and she knew just what he must be like: a bookish, bespectacled man – "a good business head, he has; clever with figures", her grandfather had always said. And something of a dandy – "Fascinated by him, the women are!" Jebediah had crowed. "And he's just as fascinated by them!"

Rebecca smiled at the thought of this bright, clever man, who was polished in his address, adept at making himself agreeable, and dressed in the latest style. She would very much like to meet him! But she would have to wait, because at the moment he was abroad on business.

She was brought out of her thoughts by the carriage rolling to a halt.

'Are we there already?' asked Rebecca.

She was surprised at the shortness of the journey.

'Yes,' said Hetty, climbing out of the carriage. 'We're here.'

Rebecca looked up at the lawyer's office building. It was decent and respectable; prosperous, even. Mr Wesley was evidently good at his job.

The two ladies were admitted to the building by a clerk.

'If you would care to follow me?' he said, with a low bow.

He was really rather an oily youth, with a manner that was an unpleasant mixture of servility and arrogance, and Rebecca could see why her grandfather had not liked lawyer's offices. But fortunately the lawyer himself was of a different stamp, and with him was her uncle Charles.

Charles Marsden was a distinguished-looking gentleman. A light smattering of grey marked his hair at the temples. His figure was, perhaps, running a little to fat, but he still cut a fine figure in his tailcoat and breeches.

'I'm so pleased you've arrived,' he said. 'Hetty was worried when you didn't get here last night, but I knew you would find the journey difficult in all this snow.'

'It was,' Rebecca acknowledged. 'I will tell you all about it later.'

He nodded. Now was not the time for conversation. Now was the time for attending to business.

Rebecca turned her attention to the lawyer. He was a small man with sparse hair and thin hands. He was dressed conservatively in a dark coat and knee breeches. On the end of his nose he wore a pair of *pince-nez*.

'Now we are all gathered together, please, take a seat,' he said.

He spoke in a dry, desiccated voice that matched his appearance perfectly.

Rebecca divested herself of her bonnet and cloak, then settled herself on a Hepplewhite chair. Hetty and Charles, similarly shedding their outdoor clothes, seated themselves on an ugly but comfortable sofa.

'Mr Kelling will be joining us?' asked Mr Wesley.

'Unfortunately not,' said Charles. 'He is at present abroad. I wrote to him, telling him of Jebediah's death, but the letter must not have reached him. I have received no reply.'

'My own efforts to contact him have met with a similar lack of success. Well, as he cannot be with us, I suggest we get down to business.'

'Indeed,' said Charles.

'Good. Then if you are all quite ready, I will begin.'

Rebecca settled herself more comfortably then turned with interest to the lawyer.

Mr Wesley cleared his throat then picked up an important-looking document that was placed in front of him. He shuffled it between his hands. In precise, dry tones he began to read.

'"This is the last will and testament of Jebediah Marsden",' he said. His voice took on a declaiming quality. '"To my only living son, Charles Marsden, I leave —"'

At that moment there was a commotion from out in the hall, and the sound of the unctuous clerk saying, 'You can't go in,' before the door was flung open, and there, on the threshold, was . . . the leonine gentleman!

He was looking even more impressive than Rebecca remembered him. His mane of dark blond hair was gleaming in a shaft of sunlight. His jaw line, devoid of the stubble that had adorned it the previous evening, was revealed in all its strength. The planes of his cheekbones, now that his hair had been brushed back from his face, were even sharper than she had remembered them, and his lips were full and firm. His clothes were immaculate. Beneath his many-caped greatcoat Rebecca glimpsed a blue tailcoat and cream breeches, pulled tight across his powerful thighs, and beneath them a pair of highly polished black boots.

But what is he doing here? thought Rebecca.

Her question was quickly answered. Charles, starting up, said warmly, 'Joshua!'

Joshua? thought Rebecca in astonishment.

This was Joshua?

No. It couldn't be.

He was the complete opposite of the picture she had built up in her mind. Where was the dandy she had imagined? True, his clothes were in the height of fashion, but he wore them with an air of wildness that spoke of plains and prairies rather than drawing-rooms. And as for being able to make himself agreeable . . . !

'Joshua!' cried Hetty with pleasure. 'We had given up all hope! How wonderful to see you again.'

Rebecca felt distinctly uncomfortable, wondering what he would say when he turned his head and saw her. If he mentioned the incident, she couldn't bear to think of Hetty's horrified response!

'And now you must meet Jebediah's granddaughter,' said Charles jovially. 'Miss Foster, this is Mr Kelling.'

Joshua turned towards her, and a humorous light brightened his copper-coloured eyes.

'Oh, Charles, for heaven's sake!' Hetty threw up her hands in despair. 'There will be no standing on ceremony between Jebediah's loved ones.' She took the introductions into her own hands. 'Joshua, this is Rebecca, and Rebecca, this is Joshua.'

Joshua took her hand, and to her annoyance Rebecca felt herself flush. But she need not have worried. Although the gleam did not leave his eye, he behaved in exemplary fashion, bowing politely over her hand. For a moment she thought he was going to kiss it . . . and gave a sigh of relief when he did not. She had the uneasy feeling that the feel of his lips on the back of her hand would have been intoxicating, and she did not want to find herself attracted to this impossible man.

As he relinquished her hand she felt her pulse begin to steady and was able to reply coolly. 'Joshua.' She inclined her head.

Fortunately, neither Hetty nor Charles had noticed the strained nature of their greeting, but she still could not be comfortable as she again took her seat. She had no idea whether Joshua would reveal they had met, or whether he would reveal the details of their meeting.

'I will begin again,' said Mr Wesley, once Joshua had shrugged himself out of his greatcoat, and they had all settled. He turned to Joshua. 'I had just begun to read Jebediah Marsden's will,' he explained.

Joshua nodded. 'Charles wrote and told me of Jebediah's death.' His face became more serious, and Rebecca realized that for all his untamed appearance he was capable of strong attachments, for it was obvious he had loved her grandfather deeply. 'I would have been here sooner but the letter was delayed and my own journey home was hampered by a bad crossing and then all this snow.'

'Quite.' Mr Wesley picked up the will once more. '"This is the last will and testament of Jebediah Marsden",' he began again. '"To my only living son, Charles Marsden, I leave the bulk of my estate."'

Charles, who had been perched on the edge of the sofa, let out a sigh of relief, and Hetty smiled happily.

Rebecca, too, was pleased. She was beginning to feel a little more comfortable. Joshua had settled himself at the other side of the room, and she was able to think clearly again.

Mr Wesley went on to give details of Charles's inheritance: a number of London properties, a variety of stocks and bonds, as well as assorted bank balances and a collection of lesser items. Then he continued. 'There are also a number of smaller legacies, as I expect you anticipated.' He cleared his throat again and went on.

"'To Miss Louisa Stanhope, I leave the sum of five thousand pounds.'"

Louisa was Rebecca's middle-aged cousin. The two of them lived together in Cheshire but Louisa had been prevented from travelling to London by her rheumatism.

Five thousand pounds was a generous sum. It would enable Cousin Louisa to indulge in a number of the luxuries she presently deprived herself of. Perhaps she could even visit Bath or Harrogate to take the waters.

Rebecca turned her attention back to Mr Wesley.

"'To my godson, Joshua Kelling",' he went on, '"I leave my signet ring —"'

Rebecca nodded thoughtfully. It seemed fitting, as well as practical, that Joshua should inherit her grandfather's ring, which was embossed with the letter *J*.

'" — together with a half share in Marsden mill".'

Rebecca glanced at Joshua. As she took in the ruthless line of his jaw she set her chin. This was an unforeseen complication: not that Joshua was to inherit half of the mill, as her grandfather had always told her that that would happen, but that Joshua was a strong and powerful man, instead of the malleable dandy she had hoped he would be.

The question now was, although she had known that Joshua was to inherit half of the mill, had he known that she was to inherit the other half?

She felt her spirit rise up inside her. She would soon find out.

"'To my beloved granddaughter, Rebecca,"' went on Mr Wesley, 'I leave my fob watch, in memory of the pleasure she gave me when she was learning to tell the time . . . and a half share in Marsden mill."'

She saw Hetty and Charles turn towards her in surprise, but it was Joshua's face that most interested her. As her eyes were drawn to his she saw his brows shoot up in surprise, before a ruthless smile curved his lip. He turned towards her and she shivered as she felt the full force of his personality being brought to bear on her. His eyes looked deep into her own, and she saw them gleam, predatory, in the winter sunlight. But if he was challenging her, then so be it, she thought. He would not find her wanting.

At the sight of her straightening her spine, an appreciative quirk touched the corner of his mouth, then he turned his attention back to Mr Wesley.

There were a few further legacies and bequests, then Mr Wesley folded the document and put it down on the table.

'That concludes the reading of the will. Are there any questions?'

He looked from one to the other of them.

None were forthcoming.

Charles stood up. 'Thank you, Wesley,' he said. 'It was good of you to take the time to see us. But now I believe we must keep you no longer. If I could trouble you to have your clerk hail us a hansom? It was too cold for our carriage to wait.'

'At once.' Mr Wesley summoned his clerk, and sent the oily youth to perform the task.

'You'll return with us, I hope, and join us for dinner, Joshua?' asked Hetty, turning with a smile towards him. 'It has been such a long time since we have seen you. We are longing for you to tell us all about your trip.'

Joshua smiled down at Hetty. To her surprise, Rebecca saw that it was a warm smile, untinged with mockery or wickedness as it was when he smiled at her. It warmed his eyes, making them glow tawny.

'I'd like to, but unfortunately I have one or two urgent matters to attend to.'

Rebecca breathed a sigh of relief.

'Then you will at least join us for tea?' Hetty pressed him.

Rebecca held her breath.

By accident, he caught sight of her and a provoking smile curved his mouth. 'Thank you. I'd be delighted.'

Rebecca fumed. He had done it on purpose, she was sure of it. It seemed he meant to make her uncomfortable for the rest of the afternoon!

'Good,' said Hetty delightedly.

Whilst they waited for a hansom, Charles and Hetty fell into an animated conversation about their good fortune. Not wishing to intrude upon them, Rebecca withdrew to the far side of the room.

To her discomfiture, Joshua followed her. 'I take it you have no objection to me joining you for tea?' he said, with a quirk at the corner of his mouth.

Rebecca fought down the urge to rise to his bait, and replied coolly, 'Of course not. What possible objection could I have?'

He shrugged his broad shoulders. 'We didn't part on the best of terms, and I wouldn't want to make you uncomfortable. If you are worried that I will mention the incident, you may rest easy. It reflects well on neither of us.'

'Nothing you could do would be important enough to make me uncomfortable,' returned Rebecca aloofly.

'No?' His eyes were mocking.

'No,' she said with spirit.

'I am glad to hear it.'

The atmosphere grew suddenly thick, and she was uncomfortably aware of a tingling sensation running down her spine. He was a formidable man, and she was beginning to see why her grandfather had said he was such a strong player in business matters. It was not because he had a head for figures - although he was undoubtedly intelligent - but because he had a ruthless streak that would serve him well in the cut and thrust of commerce. It was in his eyes, a ruthlessness that was akin to a jungle cat regarding its prey; because despite his civilised veneer there was definitely something predatory about Joshua Kelling.

And he was to be her partner in the mill.

She felt a brief moment of panic, before her spirit rose to the challenge. Here was a man against whom she could test her mettle, and that was something she did not meet with every day.

'Wondering how strong I am, Rebecca?' he asked, as if reading her mind.

'I — ' she said, startled. 'How did you know what I was thinking?' she asked accusingly.

He laughed. 'Jebediah used to wonder the same thing. We had many battles. Most of which I won. But not all.' He looked at her critically. 'You are very like him. When we met in *The Queen's Head* I wondered who you reminded me of, and now I know. When you lift your chin - yes, like that!' he said, as she unconsciously lifted it, sensing a challenge, 'then you are just like Jebediah. Not physically, of course,' he said with a wicked smile. 'But there is something about your manner, as if you are saying, Do your worst, it won't be enough, no man will ever get the better of me.' His smile broadened into sardonic laughter. 'With his blood in your veins it's no wonder you were capable of standing up to me. What is a wonder is that you didn't turn me out of the room!'

Again, that humour in his eyes. In other circumstances she would have found it appealing, but Joshua was a strong adversary and she knew she must give him no quarter. So instead of laughing, she said with deceptive mildness, 'You find it amusing that I was forced to spend the night in the attic with my maid?'

He shrugged.

'No. I don't. If I'd known who you were I'd have let you have the room. But as matters stood —'

'As matters stood?' she asked with a lift of her eyebrows.

Wishing a moment later that she hadn't. Because his face lit up with another smile. He was clearly recalling that, as matters stood, he had asked her to share his bed!

Fortunately, at that moment the unctuous clerk returned.

'I have secured you a hansom,' he said ingratiatingly, bowing to Charles and Joshua in turn before smirking at the ladies.

'Thank you,' said Charles briefly.

To Rebecca's relief, Charles gave her his arm and the two of them went out to the hansom, leaving Hetty and Joshua to follow on behind.

'What a surprise, Jebediah leaving you half the mill,' said Charles to Rebecca. Once back in Sloane Street, the four of them enjoyed a refreshing cup of tea.

'Actually, no.' Rebecca set her cup down in its porcelain saucer. 'I knew he intended to leave it to me.'

She saw Joshua's eyebrows raise at this, and was now certain that he had been unaware of Jebediah's plans. Still, he had taken the news very well, she thought.

'I will, of course, buy you out,' he remarked, joining in the conversation for the first time.

Ah! So that was why he had taken it so well! He thought it was no more than a minor disturbance of his plans. Well, he was about to find out his mistake.

'Thank you, but I have no intention of selling.'

'You won't get a better price from anyone else. I would expect you to take advice on what your half is worth, and I would give it to you without haggling. You have only to —'

At that moment the door opened and Canning, the butler, entered the room. 'Mr Munce is here,' he told Charles. 'You asked to be informed the moment he arrived.'

'Yes, thank you, Canning,' said Charles. 'Will you excuse me?' he asked. 'I have some urgent business to take care of. I won't be long.'

He left the room.

'I hope he remembers to —' began Hetty. She put down her cup with a clatter. 'I had better remind him. Will you excuse me?'

She stood up.

'Charles?' she called, following him out of the room. 'Remember to tell Mr Munce that —'

What Charles was to tell Mr Munce was lost as Hetty's voice faded away down the corridor.

Joshua, who had risen on Hetty's departure, sat down again. Returning to his conversation with Rebecca he said, 'You have only to name your price, and I will buy you out at once.'

'That is very generous of you,' remarked Rebecca, feeling strangely unsettled now that she was alone with Joshua. Although his large body was relaxed, there was definitely something uncivilized about him, but she must not let him know that she was uneasy, for he would be sure to exploit any signs of weakness. So steeling her nerve she said firmly, 'It is not for sale.'

'You can't have a half share in a mill,' he said with a look of tolerant amusement. 'It's impossible. You're a woman —'

'I believe Grandfather was aware of the fact,' she remarked.

'I'm not unaware of it myself.' His eyes became sharply focused and trailed over her body, making her feel restless and hot. She unfolded her fan and wafted it in front of her in an effort to cool herself down.

As if the action had reminded him that he was in Hetty and Charles's drawing-room, and with Jebediah's granddaughter, Joshua's eyes returned to her face. 'A half share in a mill is worthless to you,' he said reasonably. 'I'll pay you a handsome price, and you can put the money to better use.'

'No.' She shook her head. 'If Grandfather had wanted me to have money he would have left me money, but he didn't. He wanted me to have half of the mill and I intend to keep it.' She looked at him defiantly.

He returned her look levelly. 'Are you always so stubborn?' he asked. He crossed one booted foot negligently over the other and settled more comfortably in his Hepplewhite chair, resting his arm along its back.

'Stubborn?' Her eyes opened wide. 'I am not stubborn.'

'Oh, but you are. You refused to give up your room at the inn without a struggle, and now that I am offering to buy your share in the mill you have dug in your heels and refuse to sell. Tell me, Rebecca, do you ever agree to anything?'

'Of course,' she returned.

'Name it,' he said with a sardonic smile.

'Really, this is ridiculous,' she said, opening her fan again. 'I fought for my room for very good reasons, and I am refusing to sell you my share for reasons which are equally sound.' Her words were common sense personified, but she was growing more and more unsettled under his gaze.

'I cannot force you to sell —' he remarked with a lift of his eyebrows.

'Then at least we are agreed on something,' she interjected.

He gave a wry smile, but then his mouth became ruthless again. 'But if you change your mind, just let me know.' His voice took on a new, more practical, quality. 'In the meantime, I will of course keep you updated on everything of importance that happens with regard to the mill —'

'That won't be necessary,' Rebecca interrupted him. She was annoyed at his assumption that she did not mean to involve herself in her inheritance. 'I mean to take an interest in the mill myself.'

'Of course you do,' he acknowledged. 'Which is why I'll send you regular reports.'

'No.' She looked him in the eye. 'I mean that I intend to visit the mill and learn how it operates personally.'

Joshua shook his head. 'That will not be suitable.'

'Not suitable?' she enquired, trying to tear her eyes from his mane of hair, which was rippling in the most distracting way. 'I beg to differ.'

He regarded her sardonically. 'Do you, indeed?'

Rebecca felt her heart skip a beat. There was a challenging look in his eyes which made her intensely aware of the fact that they were alone.

As if realizing that the atmosphere was becoming dangerous he said, 'Young ladies are not meant to take an interest in trade.'

Rebecca had the distinct impression that he had deliberately kept his voice light in an effort to restore their conversation to more normal levels, and in an effort to break the tension that had suddenly entered the atmosphere. She was grateful for it. Her conversations with Joshua seemed to be charged with a powerful force that lay just beneath the surface. It made her skin tingle in the most alarming, and yet enlivening, way.

'Besides,' he remarked reasonably, 'mills are not very pleasant places.'

The door opened and Charles entered the room.

'Tell her, Charles,' he said, appealing to Rebecca's uncle. 'Mills are no places for women. They are always noisy and frequently very hot.'

'That's true,' said Charles judiciously. 'They are not very nice places to be, Rebecca.'

'That is not what Grandfather thought.' Her face broke into a sudden smile as she remembered his exact words. They had been sitting in his study when he had told her about the mill. She had been kneeling beside him, and he had been stroking her hair. She went on, '"You're a clever, puss, Rebecca," - that's what he used to say to me. "You'll never be content with knitting by the fire, so I'm going to leave you something to get your teeth into."'

Joshua laughed. 'Jebediah was a rogue.' Then he frowned. 'Even so, I'm surprised he left you part of the mill. He knew the dangers that were involved.'

'I am not afraid of risking an accident,' she said. 'Accidents can happen anywhere.'

'Those aren't the dangers I'm talking about.'

Rebecca was about to enquire further, but at that moment the door opened again and Hetty entered the room.

'Well, that is all sorted out.'

Joshua was about to speak, and then seemed to change his mind as to what he was going to say.

'Good.' He stood up. 'Thank you for the tea, it was delicious, Hetty, as always! But now I must be going.'

'Oh! And you only just seem to have arrived,' said Hetty. 'But never mind,' she said, brightening. 'We will see you at Lady Cranston's ball?'

'Only if Rebecca will promise me the first dance.' He turned to Rebecca with a provoking gleam in his eye.

Rebecca was torn between a desire to give him a set down and a desire to be in his arms.

'You are too courteous,' she said.

'Am I?' he asked. Adding enigmatically, 'We shall see.'

He kissed her hand and then took his leave.

His kiss had left a burning imprint, and involuntarily Rebecca looked down, half expecting to see that her glove had been scorched. But seeing that it was undamaged she shook such foolish fancies away. Joshua Kelling was the godson of her grandfather, but nothing more. It was true that she found him interesting, she told herself. But that was all.

Even so, as she joined Hetty and Charles in talking over their good fortune, she found she could not drive Joshua's image from her mind. It was there when she looked around the elegant drawing-room, hovering before her mind's eye: his mane of hair, his broad shoulders, and his copper-coloured eyes.

It was there when she looked into the fire, dancing in the burning flames.

And it was there when she laid her head on her pillow and settled down to sleep.

Chapter Three

Rebecca lifted the ruby necklace out of its box, remembering how much her mother had loved it. It was from her mother that Rebecca had inherited her distinctive colouring, and the rubies, which she had inherited on her mother's death, set it off to perfection. The warm red glow of the jewels brought out the red of her lips and added a warm glow to her porcelain-white skin.

Susan fastened it round her neck, then helped her to put on the matching ruby ear-rings.

'Oh, they're beautiful, Rebecca!' exclaimed Hetty as she bustled in. 'And how well they go with your gown. I have always liked you in red, and that gown, with its ruby bodice and white satin skirt, is so becoming! The gentlemen will think so, too, I am sure.'

Rebecca's mouth quirked. Her aunt was the best of women, but she had a habit of trying to find Rebecca a husband whenever she visited the capital. It was useless for Rebecca to protest that she did not want to marry; that she had never met a man who had made her long to join her life to his; and that until she did she was content to remain on the shelf. Her aunt could only see that she was three-and-twenty, and unwed.

Rebecca picked up her fan and gave her aunt an affectionate kiss on the cheek. She could not prevent Hetty's innocent scheming, and she knew she must accept it as an inalienable part of her aunt. Besides, thought Rebecca, perhaps it was a good thing. Ever since meeting Joshua she had felt unsettled, and she wondered whether it was Nature's way of telling her that she had, after all, been too long on the shelf.

A small voice inside her told her it had more to do with Joshua's challenging character and mane of hair - hair which inexplicably tempted her to run her fingers through it - but she refused to listen to that voice and wisely ignored it. Joshua may be unsettling and strangely attractive, but he was also entirely impossible and not at all the sort of man she would want to marry.

She recalled her wandering thoughts and followed her aunt downstairs.

'You remember Lady Cranston?' asked Hetty as, half an hour later, they arrived at that lady's splendid London home.

'Yes. I often met her at Grandfather's,' said Rebecca. She, Hetty and Charles made their way inside and slowly mounted the magnificent staircase as they waited to be received.

Lady Cranston had been a friend of Rebecca's grandfather. In her youth Lady Cranston had been plain Mary Smithers, and had lived next door to Jebediah, which was how they had come to know each other. And how Hetty and Charles now found themselves invited to her balls.

'She knows you are staying with us at the moment, Rebecca, and has invited several gentlemen she would like you to meet.'

Rebecca caught Charles's eye and they both smiled.

'Your aunt won't be happy until I've walked you down the aisle,' said Charles with a laugh.

They reached the top of the staircase where they were greeted by Lord and Lady Cranston, sparing Rebecca from the need to reply. For whilst she could not object to the good-natured efforts of her friends on her behalf, she found the gentlemen she met in Society's ballrooms to be insipid. Their lives were so ordered and well-established that there was no room in them for the challenge and stimulation Rebecca needed. Though gently bred she had inherited much of Jebediah's drive and she knew she could never be content with leading a life that offered her nothing but endless frivolity.

Having been received, they went through into the ballroom.

'What a wonderful room,' sighed Hetty as she looked around the impressive apartment.

It was indeed wonderful. Everything about it was grand. Its proportions were generous, and its high ceiling was painted with classical scenes. Sparkling chandeliers winked and shone in the candlelight; candelabras were placed on stands between each of the gilded mirrors that ran down either side of the room, and the reflected light was dazzling. But it was not the room, however grand, that caught Rebecca's attention. It was the figure of Joshua, standing at the far end.

He was talking to a handsome woman with Titian hair and green eyes who was dressed in an exquisite gown of emerald green silk. He was smiling, evidently amused by her company, which, judging from her elegance and poise, was sophisticated and witty.

Rebecca looked away . . . only to be confronted by a row of the same images stretching away into the distance, reflected in the mirrors that lined the room.

She turned away again, resolutely fixing her eyes on the orchestra, but she could not help noticing how fine Joshua was looking in the brief second before she averted her gaze. His hair had been brushed into some semblance of order, its dark blond contrasting with the black of his coat, the whiteness of his lawn shirt and the light bronze of his skin.

She had turned away just in time. As though he had felt her eyes on him he looked towards her. Even though she had looked away she was aware of him, and could not help noticing him out of the corner of her eye. She saw him make his excuses to the handsome woman, and then walk towards her across the ballroom. She felt her heart begin to beat more rapidly, but, determined not to watch him cross the room, she paid attention to her fellow guests. Despite the snowy weather and the unfashionable time of year the ball was reasonably well attended, and the varied guests seemed to be enjoying themselves.

'Ah! Here is Joshua,' said Hetty in a pleased voice, catching sight of him as he threaded his way through the other guests.

Rebecca, by now in control of herself, greeted him politely, and Hetty and Charles did the same.

'You haven't forgotten your promise?' he said teasingly to Rebecca as he stopped in front of her.

She looked up at him with an arch smile. 'No indeed.'

'Good. The first dance is about to begin.'

He gave her his arm and led her out onto the floor.

To her disappointment, the first dance was a country dance. She had hoped it might be a waltz. The dance was becoming permissible in polite society, but although she knew the steps she had never yet danced it at a ball. To have danced it for the first time with Joshua would have been interesting indeed.

' . . . not too crowded.'

With a start she realized that Joshua was speaking.

By the look in his eye she could tell he guessed she had been day-dreaming. She was just pleased that he did not know what about!

'No,' she said, accurately guessing that he had said the ballroom was not too crowded. 'At least not yet. We should have plenty of room for our steps.'

The orchestra played the opening chords and she curtseyed demurely to Joshua. In return he made her a bow.

He took her hand for the first part of the dance. This time, his touch did not burn her, but instead she felt a shiver spread up her arm.

How contrary! To find herself attracted to the most infuriating man she had ever met.

She cast about in her mind for some topic of conversation that would keep her mind from wandering down disturbing channels. The sight of a militiaman in uniform made her recall Joshua's warning the previous day that mills were dangerous places. She wondered whether he could have been referring to the problems caused by the Luddites, for they had been active in recent years.

Yes, the Luddites were a suitable choice of conversation. Talking about them would most certainly prevent her thoughts from wandering down hopelessly inappropriate paths!

The steps of the dance parted them for a minute, but when they met again Rebecca said, 'You were speaking of the dangers concerned with running the mill yesterday. Were you thinking of the Luddites?' she asked.

Joshua gave a wry smile, as though guessing the reason for her unusual choice of conversation.

But no. Of course he could not have done. She was letting her imagination run away with her - again.

Whatever his thoughts, he fell in with her choice of conversation. 'Yes. I was.'

'Have there been any problems with them at Marsden mill?'

'No. Marsden mill was never attacked. But that doesn't mean that we can relax in our vigilance. These are turbulent times, and we need to remember it.' The steps of the dance parted them again, but when they came together, Joshua asked, 'Your grandfather spoke to you about the Luddite problem, I take it?'

'No,' said Rebecca.

'Then you don't know the kind of havoc they can cause,' he frowned.

'On the contrary,' she informed him. 'I know only too well. Cousin Louisa and I live in Cheshire, as you know. That is very close to the source of many of the problems. The Luddites have caused a lot of difficulties in the north of England recently, and in the Midlands as well.' Her mouth quirked humorously. 'Despite being a mere woman, I have been known to read a newspaper from time to time,' she said with a sideways glance.

He laughed. But then his expression became more serious. 'Reading a newspaper is one thing; running a mill is another. I wasn't exaggerating when I said that mills are dangerous places. If you read the newspapers, you know that what I am saying is true.'

'I know it was true,' said Rebecca. 'There has been a lot of unrest, but it is over now. The ringleaders have been dealt with and that has put a stop to it.'

'Unfortunately it may not be as simple as that. Although a lot of the Luddite ringleaders have been dealt with, the underlying problems haven't gone away, and trouble could break out again at any time. We will not know if the Luddite movement has really been broken until we have had at least two or three peaceful years. There is still a lot of resentment against the using of machines because the machines take away men's jobs, and without jobs they can't feed their families.'

'In that I have a great deal of sympathy for them,' said Rebecca. She looked at him challengingly as she walked down the room beside him, her hand raised and joined to his. 'I warn you, if you mean to put men out of work then I will do everything in my power to thwart you.'

'It would not surprise me,' he returned, with a flash in his copper-coloured eyes.

And oh! how they sent shivers through her, those eyes, she thought, as she turned away from him, in accordance with the dance. Why could they not have been green, or blue, or grey, or anything but copper?

The dance brought them together again.

'I can understand why the men hate machines,' continued Rebecca. She was determined not to succumb to the magnetism of the man before her. If she did that, he would surely relegate her, as a mere woman, to a subordinate role, and forbid her any real influence over her inheritance.

But she was determined to play her part. Although she knew very little about running a mill she meant to use her part-ownership to make sure that the men and women who worked there did not suffer the draconian working conditions that were prevalent in some mills.

This, she suspected, was the part her grandfather had meant her to play, bringing a softening influence to Joshua's hard and predatory nature.

'The machines take away their jobs. I am not surprised they're resentful.'

'Being resentful is one thing,' he remarked. 'Being violent is quite another. The Luddites are no respecters of persons. If they feel their livelihoods are threatened they are not above breaking into the homes of mill owners and holding them at gunpoint.'

'You are thinking of James Balderstone,' said Rebecca. The assault on James Balderstone had been in all the newspapers at the time. His house had been broken into by a mob, and he had been held at gunpoint by a number of Luddites whilst their fellows had smashed up one of his frames.

'Among others. And in some cases the situation has been even worse. In Stockport, a mob broke into one of the mills and destroyed the looms before turning their attention to the owner's house and setting it on fire.'

'Nevertheless, I intend to take an interest in my inheritance,' said Rebecca firmly. 'Grandfather left me half the mill for a purpose and I don't want to let him down. Besides, he is right. I can't be content with sitting by the fire and knitting! I long for a challenge. I am too much like him to be content with idling my life away.'

To her surprise, she saw a look of respect and understanding cross Joshua's face. But then it disappeared, and she could tell that, no matter how much he might understand her feelings, he was not about to give in. He did not want a woman as a partner, and it would take more than a flash of respect to change his mind.

There was no time for anything further, however. The dance was drawing to its close. The last chords sounded and she turned to Joshua and dropped him a curtsey.

He made her a bow and then, offering her his arm, he escorted her to the side of the room. Hetty was waiting for them. The three of them enjoyed a little light conversation before Joshua made his excuses and left their side.

'My, you made a handsome couple,' said Hetty, unfolding her fan and wafting it in front of her face to create a cooling breeze. 'It's such a pity that Joshua is too young to marry.' She gave a sigh. 'He has too much drive and ambition to settle down. Perhaps, when he is older, and needs to set up his nursery . . . But never mind, there are plenty of eligible bachelors here tonight. Oh, look, here is Lord Henderton.' She caught sight of Rebecca's humorous expression and said ruefully, 'I know you don't like me to play the part of the matchmaker, Rebecca, but I would so like to see you settled.'

'I promise you that if I ever fall in love I will be happy to marry,' she said. 'But not until.'

'Well, I can ask for no more than that,' said Hetty. She turned towards the young nobleman. 'Ah! Lord Henderton! How lovely to see you. I don't believe you know my niece.'

Lord Henderton professed himself eager to rectify that sad state of affairs, and before long Rebecca found him leading her out onto the floor. Lord Henderton turned out to be a good dancer and an agreeable companion, and she enjoyed the cotillion they danced together.

Hetty nobly refrained from asking her how she had found Lord Henderton when the dance came to an end, but Rebecca took pity on her, telling her that she had found him most agreeable.

'And there are a number of other young gentlemen here tonight who are equally agreeable,' said Hetty, eager to promote Rebecca's happiness. 'You must let me introduce you to Mr Porter.' She wafted her fan in the direction of the gentleman in question. 'He comes from a very good family, and his mother and I are old friends.'

Rebecca allowed Hetty to make the introduction, and then accepted Mr Porter's hand for the next dance. Like Lord Henderton, he was a pleasant and agreeable companion, but he was looking for a meek and biddable wife. Besides, his closeness did not make her skin tingle . . .

After Mr Porter, Rebecca danced with a succession of pleasant and agreeable young men.

It was whilst she was dancing with Mr Yunge, however, that she became aware of another gentleman watching her with a puzzled expression. As soon as the dance ended he accosted her, saying, 'Haven't we met somewhere before?'

Rebecca took in his bland, slack-featured face and shook her head. 'I don't believe so.' Then, remembering that Joshua had been reminded of her grandfather on first meeting her, she said, 'Perhaps you knew my grandfather, Jebediah Marsden. There is a family resemblance, I believe.'

He shook his head. 'No, I never knew Jebediah Marsden.' He regarded her closely. 'It was somewhere recently that I saw you, I am certain. You have been in London for the winter?'

'No. I have only just arrived.'

'And you are sure we have never met?' he asked curiously.

'Positive.' Rebecca was firm.

He gave a sigh. 'I could have sworn . . . oh, well I dare say it will come back to me.'

Rebecca murmured a polite nothing and returned to Hetty's side.

'I am glad you are getting to know some of the gentlemen here,' said Hetty, rather anxiously, 'but if I can just give you a word of warning, Rebecca. The gentleman you were talking to just now - the slack-featured gentleman, George Lacy - he is not quite the thing.'

'Don't worry aunt,' teased Rebecca. 'I promise not to form a *tendre* for him!'

To Rebecca's surprise, Hetty did not smile at her sally.

'That isn't what I mean,' said Hetty, shaking her head. 'He has a malicious nature, and he delights in inflicting harm. He loves nothing better than to gossip - I declare he is worse than a woman in that way - and if he ever discovers something any decent person would keep quiet about, he noises it abroad. Oh! Not openly. That would be too dangerous for him. There are still gentlemen who are prepared to fight a duel if they feel their own of their wife's honour has been called into question. But nevertheless he finds a way of making it known.'

'Never fear,' said Rebecca. 'He cannot hurt me. I have nothing to hide.'

'Even so, I would rather you kept away from him,' said Hetty, worried.

'I shall do as you suggest,' said Rebecca. She had detected something underhand about Mr Lacy herself, and was happy to assure Hetty she had no intention of cultivating his acquaintance.

'Good.' Hetty was satisfied. 'Oh, look,' she said. 'Here is Joshua. I believe he means to ask you for another dance.'

Rebecca felt her heart skip a beat. Dancing with Joshua had been enlivening the first time, but she did not trust herself to accept his hand for a second time. She must think of some excuse.

'May I have the honour of your hand for the next dance?' asked Joshua as he joined them at the side of the ballroom.

'I must beg to be excused,' Rebecca said. 'I am feeling rather hot.'

'Indeed.' His eyes fixed on hers and held them for a long moment.

If she had not been hot before, she certainly was now!

As if convinced that she was indeed feeling heated by the delicate flush that sprang to her cheek, Joshua released her from his gaze, saying, 'Then you must let me fetch you an ice.'

Rebecca accepted his offer and he strode off, to return a few minutes later with a refreshing confection.

By this time Hetty was deep in conversation with one of the other matrons, leaving Rebecca feeling vulnerable. As she took the ice she decided it was best to retreat once more into general conversation. She was just about to launch into a discussion of the war against France, asking Joshua whether he felt that Napoleon was indeed close to ultimate defeat, as the newspapers suggested, when she became aware of George Lacy's eyes on them.

'What is it?' asked Joshua, seeing her frown.

'That gentleman,' said Rebecca, her hand poised halfway to her mouth. 'George Lacy. He is watching me.'

'That's hardly surprising,' said Joshua. His eyes warmed as they roved over her face, taking in her bright eyes and her naturally red lips, before dropping to her delicious curves, which were encased in her satin gown.

Rebecca blushed. 'You must not say such things to me!' she reprimanded him.

He looked down at her more intently, and the mocking smile left his lips. 'Why not, when they are true?' he asked.

Rebecca could think of no answer to this. Even so, she wished he would not say such things, or look at her in such a disturbing way. She was becoming prey to certain unsettling images, images of him sweeping her into his arms and kissing her on the lips.

'Tell me,' she said, striving to turn the conversation into less disturbing channels, and falling back on her earlier idea of discussing Napoleon. 'What do you think of Napoleon's chances, now that so many countries have entered a coalition against him?'

'Determined to talk of commonplaces?' he asked with a quizzical look.

She could think of no suitable reply, and covered her silence by taking a spoonful of ice.

Then his quizzical look vanished, and Rebecca realized he had seen the wisdom of this himself.

'Very well,' he said. 'I think that Napoleon was a fool to invade Russia last year. I think his defeat at the Battle of the Nations in October spelt his doom, and I think the Coalition will eventually beat him. He's a great general, but not even he can stand out against Russia, Prussia, Sweden, Austria and Bavaria when they are all united against him.' He gave a wry smile, then said unexpectedly, 'I also think his defeat will be very bad for business.'

Rebecca was startled. 'Bad for business?'

Joshua nodded. 'Supplying the army with the material for their uniforms has been very lucrative for the mills.'

Rebecca laughed. 'Do you ever stop thinking of business?' she asked.

'Not often.'

She smiled. 'I suppose I should be pleased. It is a good trait to have in a partner.'

She finished her ice.

'You are still determined not to sell me your share of the mill?' he asked.

'I am.'

'Think it over carefully, Rebecca. Remember, the problems with the Luddites could flare up again at any time. I don't want you putting yourself in danger.'

There was a spark of something unfathomable in his eyes as he said it, and for a moment she had the wild idea that he was concerned about her.

But of course he was concerned, she reminded herself a moment later. He was concerned because she was Jebediah's granddaughter. And Joshua had been very fond of Jebediah.

'I don't intend to put myself in danger,' she reassured him, putting her empty dish on a silver tray as a footman walked by. 'But I intend to take an interest in my inheritance. You must reconcile yourself to my visiting the mill in order to acquaint myself with it.'

Joshua gave a wry smile. 'Your grandfather often spoke about you, but he neglected to tell me about your stubborn streak. It is almost as strong as my own.'

At that moment Lady Cranston approached them and introduced a nervous young lady fresh from the schoolroom. Joshua, doing his duty, fell in with Lady Cranston's unspoken wishes and politely asked the young lady to dance.

Hetty was still busy chattering to one of her friends, and seeing that she was occupied Rebecca felt free to slip out of the room. Despite her ice she was still feeling overheated and wanted to retreat to somewhere cooler and quieter for a few minutes.

It was certainly cooler in the corridor than the ballroom, but with all the candles in the magnificent chandeliers, it was still hot.

She opened one of the doors that led off from the corridor, and found herself in a small ante-room, which on closer inspection turned out to be a pretty little morning-room. A fire was lit but it was banked down. The coals showed blackly against the white marble fireplace, and the atmosphere was pleasantly cool.

Rebecca closed the door behind her. She was pleased to have found somewhere to rest, and she was relieved to be alone.

She had found being with Joshua unsettling and she was not sure that she liked the sensation. She was used to being in control of her life and her feelings, before Joshua had entered her life and disturbed everything. He was like no other man she had ever met. He was ruthless and hard in many ways, and yet there was an unmistakeable warmth underneath.

Was it the contrast between his hard surface and his inner warmth that attracted her? she wondered.

Whenever he was near her she found her thoughts wandering down new and unsettling paths, and try as she might she could not stop them.

She sighed, and wandered over to the window. She would give herself a few minutes in the morning-room to cool down and then return to the ballroom.

Looking round, she tried to find something to distract her thoughts.

Ah! A collection of miniatures. They hung next to the window, on the gold-painted wall. She moved closer to study them. They were exquisitely executed, and she was just marvelling over the detail in them when the door opened. She turned round . . . and saw George Lacy enter the room.

'Mr Lacy!' she exclaimed. She was not pleased to see him. Of all the guests at the ball, he was the one she least wanted to see. Especially now, when she had been hoping for a few minutes peace.

'Miss Foster,' he replied.

He did not seem surprised to see her. His attitude made her feel on edge. She examined him warily. Of middle height, he appeared to be about forty years of age. He was well dressed, his striped yellow waistcoat contrasting with his blue tailcoat and his white linen, but even so, there was a sharp look in his eye.

'I was just about to return to the ballroom,' she said. Her aunt's warnings were clear in her mind, and she was determined to leave the room at once. But as she passed him on the way to the door he suddenly lunged at her. His arms wrapped themselves round her like steel wires and she smelt the rancidness of his breath as he tried to fasten his mouth on hers. His action was as shocking as it was unexpected, and in horror Rebecca pushed him away.

'Come now, no need to play the innocent,' he said insinuatingly. He approached her again. 'Just a little kiss, that's all I ask.'

To her annoyance, Rebecca found that she was shaking. 'Have you taken leave of your senses?' she demanded, rapidly regaining control of herself. She drew herself up and said, with as much authority as she could muster, 'Let me pass.'

'Quite the little actress, aren't we?' he sneered. 'But I know what you really are. That virtuous pose won't wash with me.'

He lunged at her again, and this time he managed to clamp his lips to her own. She shut her mouth firmly and stamped down hard on his foot.

He let out a cry of rage. It had the fortunate effect of making his mouth leave hers, but then he lunged for her again. She backed away. She fumbled behind her in an effort to grasp one of the candlesticks that stood on the mantelpiece. It would make an effective weapon. But just as her fingers closed around it the door opened and Joshua was revealed in the doorway.

It took Joshua only a second to take in what was happening and then he was across the room and lifting Lacy bodily away from Rebecca, before turning and depositing him none too gently on the ground again. Joshua's bulk was now between Lacy and Rebecca, protecting her from any further attack.

'You're a cur, Lacy,' he said with contempt. 'I suggest you apologize to the lady at once.'

He stepped aside so that Lacy could do so, watching him all the time to make sure that he did not try to attack Rebecca again. But instead of complying, Lacy only flicked the lace at his wrists and straightened his cravat.

Then he jeered, 'Lady? Oh, no, Kelling, I don't think so.'

He looked from Joshua to Rebecca and back again. He was beginning to regain his confidence now that Joshua had let him go, and he continued more boldly. 'I knew I'd seen her somewhere before but I couldn't think where. And then it came back to me. When I saw her dancing with you, I realized I'd seen the two of you together, and then I remembered where it was. It was at *The Queen's Head*.'

Rebecca felt her spirits sink.

'Looking a bit smarter than the last time I saw you, aren't you?' sneered Lacy, warming to his theme. 'You were wearing nothing but breeches then, if I remember correctly. Not the sort of sight for a 'lady', is it, Kelling? And Rebecca . . . She was more chastely dressed, I'll admit, but I don't suppose that state of affairs existed for very long, did it? Not after I heard you asking her to share your bed. A pity I didn't get to see the finale; that would have been something! I only got to see the opening act. Still, it was enough.' He rubbed his bruised arm. 'You wanted to conduct your little affair in secret, didn't you? You thought you could go out to *The Queen's Head* and have the "lady" in your room with no one being the wiser. But you were wrong. Because I was there, Kelling, and I saw the two of you together. And what's more, before this evening's over, everyone else will know it too.'

Rebecca felt her stomach churn. Lacy had seen them together at *The Queen's Head*, when she was arguing with Joshua over the room. The door, she remembered, had been open, because she had not wanted to close it, for to do so would have been to shut herself in with a stranger. It was the worst thing that could possibly have happened. Although the encounter had been innocent, no one would believe it.

Indeed, Lacy himself did not believe it. Having seen her talking to Joshua whilst Joshua had been in a state of partial undress, and having heard Joshua invite her to share his bed, he had drawn his own conclusions. And now he meant to noise them abroad.

Her spirits sank still further as she realized that her reputation was ruined.

But she had reckoned without Joshua's strength of character.

'I don't think so.' His voice was like steel.

'Oh, don't you?' jeered Lacy. 'Well, perhaps if your mistress had been more accommodating, and perhaps if you hadn't manhandled me, then I might have been persuaded to keep what I know to myself. But as it is . . .'

His voice tailed away. He had started his speech full of confidence, but at the word "mistress" the atmosphere had changed, and a deadly silence now filled the room.

Lacy glanced nervously at Joshua and backed away.

There was a moment of tense silence. Then, 'Tell me, Lacy,' said Joshua. 'How are you with a pistol?' He spoke conversationally, but the air suddenly felt as tight as a drum, as though one wrong word or gesture would rupture it.

Lacy felt it. He fingered his collar nervously, as though he was finding it difficult to breath. 'What do you mean?'

'I mean, that if you blacken Miss Foster's name in any way, you will find yourself needing one,' said Joshua levelly.

Lacy gave a bark of laughter, but it was forced. 'You wouldn't fight a duel over her,' he said with bravado. 'She's not your wife. She's nothing but your strumpet. Besides, duels aren't for your kind.' He sneered again. 'You're in trade, Kelling. You're not even a gentleman.'

'I count four,' said Joshua calmly.

Lacy looked at him suspiciously.

'Four reasons for calling you out,' Joshua elaborated. 'One, your attack on Miss Foster; two, your threat to spread gossip about the lady and myself; three, your slur on the lady's character; and four, your slur on my right to call myself a gentleman.'

Lacy licked his lips.

'You are the only person to know of the incident at *The Queen's Head*,' went on Joshua, his eyes hard. 'If I discover that anyone else knows about it, I will know who has been spreading the rumour. And I, Lacy, am a very good shot.'

Lacy looked from one to the other of them, as if trying to decide whether it would be worth his while to resort to some kind of blackmail. But one look at Joshua's implacable features decided him. 'Very well,' he said through clenched teeth. 'I will keep quiet.'

'A wise choice,' said Joshua evenly. He strode over to the door and held it open.

Lacy, with a last furtive look, slipped out of the room.

With his departure, some of the tension that had filled the room began to dissipate. Rebecca let out sigh of relief. Without realizing it, she had been holding her breath.

Joshua, whose eyes had followed Lacy out of the room, turned to look at her.

As she felt his eyes on her, Rebecca felt suddenly awkward. He was taking in every detail of her: the flush on her cheeks; her rapid breathing; and the rise and fall of her breast.

'Did he hurt you?' he asked, his eyes returning to her own.

'No.' She remembered Lacy's attack on her, and was thankful that Joshua had arrived when he did - although she had given a good account of herself before he had entered the room. In an attempt to lighten the atmosphere, which was still tense, though now in a subtly different way, she gave a weak smile and said, 'Though I believe I hurt him. I stamped on his foot when he tried to kiss me.'

He smiled, too. Then his eyes mellowed, and the hard line of his mouth softened. 'I hope you would not stamp on my foot if —' he began; before cutting himself off.

There was a heart-stopping moment and everything was suddenly very still. Rebecca could hear the coals shifting in the hearth. As if some unseen force was compelling her to do so, she turned her eyes up to his. 'If —?' she whispered. Her voice trembled, but the rest of her was rigid. It was as though she was waiting for something. But what?

'If . . .' said Josh, his voice suddenly husky.

He was looking incredibly desirable. Standing there before her in the candlelight, with the flames painting gold highlights into his hair and with copper sparks flashing from his eyes, he was the most devastatingly attractive man Rebecca had ever seen. But it was not just his mane of dark blond hair and his copper eyes that made him so attractive, it was the force of his character; a force which echoed her own. He crossed the space between them and took her hands between his, whilst all the time his eyes never left hers. He stroked his strong fingers over the backs of her hand then turned them over and stroked the palms.

He dropped one of her hands, and she felt torn, both relieved that he had let it go, and yet devastated that he had done so.

But he kept hold of her other hand. He kissed the back of it, then stripping off her long white evening glove he kissed it again, turning it over and kissing her palm. She gave a long, shuddering sigh, and as if it released something inside him he abandoned convention entirely and pulled her roughly into his embrace.

His eyes bored down into her own. It was as though he was looking through them into her very soul. His mouth came closer and her lips began to part. She could feel the heat of his breath, clean and sweet, and her eyelids, heavy, started to close. She felt his arms drawing her closer, crushing her against him in a virile embrace; she could almost taste his lips, and then —

A loud crash from just outside the room penetrated the spellbinding aura that surrounded her. She became gradually aware that there was a world beyond the one encircled by Joshua's arms, and knew that she must rejoin it.

He knew it, too. He was pulling away from her, dropping his arms, letting her go . . . .

She swayed for a moment, not yet able to stand without his support, then made a great effort and managed to steady herself. As she did so she began to remember where she was, and to realize what had just happened.

Oh, no! she thought, overcome with mortification. Despite all her resolutions to the contrary she had almost succumbed to Joshua's powerful attraction.

'I . . . I must go,' she said, wondering what had come over her. How could she have become so lost to all sense that she would allow Joshua to pull her into his arms? She picked up her glove and pulled it on with shaking fingers. 'Hetty will be wondering where I am.'

'Of course.' His voice was husky.

To Rebecca's relief he stood aside so that she could pass.

'But you will not find Hetty in the ballroom,' he said. 'She has had to retire to the ladies withdrawing-room. Mr Korbett stood on her gown in the *boulanger* and ripped the hem. She asked me to explain her absence and tell you she will return to the ballroom as soon as her dress has been mended.'

'So that is what brought you here at such an opportune moment,' said Rebecca.

'That. Or fate.' He looked down at her with an enigmatic expression on his face.

Her eyelids drooped. The atmosphere was again becoming charged. She must leave. At once. Whilst she still could.

With a great effort she stirred herself. She gave herself a moment to gather her wits. Then, smoothing her skirt, which had become crushed when Joshua had pulled her into his arms, she went out into the hall.

As she did so she caught sight of a wisp of white muslin whisking round the corner. She noticed that one of the chairs lining the corridor was a little out of place, and guessed that one of the young ladies at the ball must have knocked it over, causing the crash she and Joshua had heard.

For a worrying moment she wondered if the young lady could have overheard her conversation with George Lacy. But then she dismissed the idea. What well bred young lady would listen at a door?

She patted her hair, unfurled her fan, and then making an effort to appear calm and unruffled, she returned to the ballroom. Just before she went in she took a moment to glance at herself in a gilded looking-glass hanging on the wall.

To her surprise - and her profound relief - no trace of what had just passed between her and Joshua could be seen. She had thought it must be clear to all the world that he had pulled her roughly into his arms, and that she had turned up her face in willing expectation of his kiss. But she looked serene. No one would guess, from looking at her, that inside, her emotions were a conflicting mass of unresolved feelings.

Why had Joshua kissed her hand? Why had he stripped off her glove? Why had she let him? Why had he dragged her into his arms? And why had she not recoiled in horror when he had done so, instead of melting into his arms as though she had been born to do it?

These were questions she could not answer. They disturbed her deeply, and shook her to the roots of everything she knew - or thought she knew - about herself.

Her aplomb was gone, leaving nothing but confusion in its wake.

But this was not the time or the place to think about it. No matter how difficult it was, she must push those thoughts aside. She took a deep breath and then she went through into the ballroom.

Fortunately she had not been missed. Hetty had not yet returned to the ballroom, and Charles was partnering an elderly dowager on the dance floor. By the time Hetty returned, Rebecca was able to laugh and dance, and it appeared as though nothing untoward had happened.

Joshua remained in the morning-room in order to give Rebecca time to rejoin their fellow guests. It would not have done for them to return together in case their joint return had given rise to speculation about their absence. The situation was difficult enough, with George Lacy having seen them together at *The Queen's Head*. The last thing Joshua wanted to do was to expose Rebecca to any more harmful gossip.

But that was not the only thought to plague him. Whilst he waited in the morning-room he asked himself what he had been thinking of in taking Rebecca into his arms. As soon as he had rescued her from the clutches of George Lacy he should have encouraged her to return to the ballroom. Instead of which he had given way to his feelings, dragging her into his embrace. It was only the timely intervention of the crash from outside the room that had prevented him from kissing her.

And oh! how he had wanted to. He had never been so tempted in all his life. It had been bad enough when he had kissed her hands - and what madness had induced him to strip off her glove? - but when he had felt her soft body pressing against him as he had embraced her, when she had turned her face up to his, the temptation had been overwhelming.

That she had not known what she was doing had been clear enough. If he had not known that she was an innocent in the ways of men and women from hearing Jebediah speak of her, he would still have recognized it for himself. She had led a protected life, and despite her spirit, her innocence was palpable. And yet when she had turned up her face it had almost undone him.

He shook his head in bewilderment. How had it happened? She roused in him feelings the like of which he had never known. Feelings that were too strong to deny.

He paced the room. His encounter with Rebecca had left him filled with a restless energy, and he needed to do something to dispel it.

He still could not believe that he had almost kissed her. If he had done so . . . .

He did not want to think about it.

Fortunately he had been saved from taking such an irrevocable step by the crash outside. Because if not for that he would have kissed her and then his fate would have been sealed. For having kissed her he would have had to offer her marriage.

Marriage!

He shuddered as he thought of it.

Marriage was not for him.

When he was eight-and-thirty, perhaps, and had a dynasty to found. But not at eight-and-twenty.

As his thoughts returned to George Lacy, however, he began to realize that he must offer her marriage anyway, whatever his personal feelings might be. Because if Lacy had seen them together at *The Queen's Head* then someone else could have seen them there as well.

He had never even considered this complication after he had spoken to her at the inn. It had never occurred to him that by being alone with her, however unwittingly, in one of *The Queen's Head*'s bedrooms, he had compromised her. And if it had occurred to him at the time he would not have cared. Rebecca had been nothing to him then; no one; and he would not have felt obliged to offer her marriage. Society, he knew, would have expected it, but he had never allowed himself to be dictated to by anyone, and certainly not by Society.

But now that he knew who she was, and realized that they had been seen, he would have to offer her marriage anyway. It was not because of Lacy - Lacy would not talk, he was too much of a coward - but someone else might have seen them, and he would do nothing to risk the reputation of Jebediah's granddaughter.

His face softened as he thought of his godfather. It was Jebediah who had supported him in his desire to learn about the cotton mills that were springing up in the north, bringing wealth to the area and the country as a whole; Jebediah who had reasoned with Joshua's family, telling them that trade did not sully the hands of a gentleman, but instead encouraged enterprise and self-reliance; and Jebediah who, sensing a kindred spirit in Joshua, comprising a ruthless determination and a sharp ambition, had helped him achieve his goals.

He owed everything he was to Jebediah. And he would not repay the old man by bringing disgrace to Rebecca.

It was a nuisance, he thought, running his hand through his mane of hair. He did not want to marry, no matter how desirable he found Rebecca. And yet it must be done. He knew where his duty lay.

What was that Hetty had said earlier in the evening? That she intended to take Rebecca to visit Frost Fair tomorrow? Very well. He would meet Rebecca there, and tell her of his plan. He and Rebecca would become betrothed. And at the earliest opportunity they would be married.

Chapter Four

'Frost Fair?' asked Rebecca.

It was the following day, and she and Hetty were sitting in the drawing-room, looking through the latest edition of the Ladies' Monthly Museum. It was one of Hetty's favourite fashion journals, and the two ladies were perusing the latest styles when Hetty mentioned the fair.

'What is Frost Fair?' Rebecca looked up from the journal. She had never heard any mention of it before, and was curious as to what it could be.

'It really is quite exciting,' said Hetty. 'I was talking to Mrs Minshull last night and she told me all about it. She and her husband have been, it seems, and they found it most exhilarating. Frost Fair is a fair set up on the Thames,' she explained, 'The weather has been so cold this winter that the river has frozen over.'

Rebecca looked at her in surprise.

'It is quite true, I assure you,' said Hetty. 'I haven't taken leave of my senses! But it is not to be wondered at that you are surprised. I was surprised myself. I do not remember the Thames ever freezing before - although I believe my mother told me about something similar happening in her childhood,' she said with a frown, as she struggled to recall the memory. 'Yes,' she said more definitely, 'I believe she did. Not that I ever saw it then, of course. But I would like to see it now. It is truly amazing, or so Mrs Minshull says. And it is not only the river that is amazing, it is what has been done to it. The shopkeepers and hawkers have lost no time in transforming it into a street - Freezewater Street, they call it. They've set up stalls and booths, and are busy selling their wares. But that is not all. There are jugglers and acrobats to entertain people, and all manner of open-air coffee shops —'

'Coffee shops?' interrupted Rebecca, growing more and more surprised.

'Yes. People have to have something hot inside them to keep out the cold,' Hetty explained.

'But surely the ice isn't strong enough to hold tables and chairs, as well as stalls and booths and people?' asked Rebecca.

'It appears to be. Apparently, it is solid. And not only tables and chairs have been set out on it, but braziers, too. There are all manner of meats and pastries for sale, and roasted chestnuts. In fact, the chestnuts are particularly good, if Mrs Minshull is to be believed.'

'Mrs Minshull is fond of chestnuts?' asked Rebecca humorously, remembering that lady's impressive girth.

Hetty's eyes twinkled. 'She is. But it is not just the stalls of food that sound so interesting, it is the host of things to do. There are skates to hire, and all kinds of other entertainments. I thought, if you liked, we could go.'

'I wouldn't miss it for the world,' said Rebecca, caught by Hetty's enthusiasm.

'Then it is settled. We will go this afternoon.'

After luncheon, wrapped up well against the cold, Rebecca, Hetty and Charles set out to visit Frost Fair. A few soft white snowflakes drifted out of the sky as they stepped into the carriage, but otherwise the day was fine. Once they were settled the carriage set off at a sedate pace. The roads were very slippery, and Charles had given his coachman instructions to take matters carefully, as he did not want to risk any injury to the horses.

London looked very different under its thick coating of snow and Rebecca barely recognised the streets. They looked strange compared to the last time she had seen them, in the summer. But it was the river that was the most startling sight. It had been completely transformed.

'It's breathtaking,' gasped Rebecca as she stepped out of the carriage once they reached the Thames. She marvelled at the change the bitterly cold weather had brought about. The river, which usually flowed merrily past, was now frozen solid. Up and down its length, boats and ships could be seen, caught fast like flies in amber, trapped until the thaw.

'It is indeed,' came a voice behind her.

Turning round she saw Joshua.

She had not been prepared for his presence, as she had not known he intended to visit the fair. As he took her hand her heart missed a beat and her wayward imagination returned to their encounter in the morning-room at Lady Cranston's ball.

With difficulty she schooled her thoughts, bringing them determinedly back to the present.

'Joshua,' said Hetty, greeting him warmly. 'What a nice surprise to find you here. Isn't it a marvellous sight?'

'It is,' he said. But instead of taking in his surroundings, his eyes lingered on Rebecca as he said it.

'I can't believe all these stalls and booths have been set up on the ice,' said Hetty as they began to walk across the frozen river, taking in the varied scene. 'I know Mrs Minshull told me all about it, but still, seeing it all is very different to hearing about it. I have never seen anything quite like it.'

Rebecca was relieved at the normality of Hetty's conversation. It drew her thoughts back to the present, and away from the disturbing aura generated by Joshua. It was an aura of strength and ruthlessness, and something more. There seemed something particular about it today, and she was pleased she was not alone with him. If she had been, she would have been even less at ease. She had the unnerving feeling there was something he wanted to say to her, and although she had no idea what it could be she guessed, from the way he was looking at her, it was something that could not be said in front of Hetty and Charles.

Endeavouring to shake off the feeling, she turned her thoughts away from Joshua and gave her attention to the scene that met her eyes. Everywhere she looked, people seemed to be enjoying themselves. Some, like her own party, were people of fashion, out unusually early in order to savour the novel experience of the Fair. Others were people from less exalted walks of life: apprentices with their sweethearts, servants on their half-day holidays, and grubby urchins revelling in the noise and confusion of the scene.

And then there were those who were making their living from the Fair: the hawkers and the piemen who walked confidently across the ice with trays of pies on their heads, and a string of stray dogs following hopefully behind them! There were stilt walkers and fire eaters who roused the admiration of the onlookers with their amazing skills; and pedlars who sold ribbons and ballad sheets from trays hung round their necks.

The scents were no less varied. The food on offer filled the air with the smell of pies and cakes, chestnuts and gingerbread, roast meat and apples.

It was a wonderful occasion.

'My dear?' said Charles, offering Hetty his arm.

Hetty took his proffered arm with alacrity, and Rebecca realized with a sinking feeling that she was going to have to take Joshua's arm.

Sure enough he offered it to her, an unfathomable gleam in his eye.

Acrobats tumbled past them as they walked across the ice. Jugglers threw multi-coloured balls into the air and caught them again, displaying their skill.

Hetty and Charles stopped to watch the printing presses turning out the latest satirical prints, making fun of the coldness of the weather. At last they all sat down at an open-air coffee house and had steaming hot drinks.

Fortified by the coffee, they risked eating slices of "Lapland Mutton" from a stall - 'although it's no more from Lapland than I am!' laughed Charles - and followed it with steaming hot rolls.

She would have been enjoying it, Rebecca thought, if not for Joshua's unsettling presence. Because, despite the fact that his nearness should mean no more to her than the nearness of any other gentleman, it was playing havoc with her insides. It kept throwing up the memory of the previous evening, when he had taken her into his arms; and the unsettling realization that, as his mouth had hovered mere inches from hers, she had wanted to feel his kiss.

Having refreshed themselves they set off again and soon came upon a stall renting out skates.

'Oh, wonderful!' exclaimed Hetty. 'It's ages since I've been skating. Do you skate, Joshua?' she asked him.

'I do.'

'Then you must skate with Rebecca,' said Hetty, 'for I am not very good at it, and I will need Charles's arm to support me.'

'It will be my pleasure,' said Joshua with a purposeful look in his eye.

Before long, Rebecca had fastened on a pair of skates and was heading out to the centre of the ice on Josh's arm. He skated well, with long, powerful strokes. Once in a clear space he drew her towards him in one smooth gesture and put his arm around her waist. Then, taking her hand he set about guiding her across the ice.

The ice was as smooth and as slippery as glass. The sweeping boys had done their jobs well, plying their birch brooms to keep it free of slush and debris, and brushing it clean of the churned-up ice the skates left in their wakes.

'Rebecca,' he said, once they were away from Hetty and Charles, 'there are things we must discuss.'

She did not know what he was going to say, but some instinct warned her not to let him say it, so she began the conversation in her own way.

'Tell me Joshua, when will you be going to Manchester? Now that you have inherited half the mill, I am sure you will want to be attending to business.'

'Trying to get rid of me, Becky?' he asked, an amused twinkle in his eye.

'Perhaps I am.'

'You won't find it so easy!' he said. But then he became serious. 'Rebecca, I was wrong to let you go last night. I shouldn't have let you return to the ballroom after our meeting in the morning-room until things had been settled between us.'

Rebecca felt her curiosity rise. Until things had been settled between them? What did he mean?

Joshua was continuing. 'I should have realized when it happened that we might have been seen together at *The Queen's Head*. As soon as I met you again I should have taken the necessary steps to protect your reputation and keep you free of the interference of people like George Lacy. However, what's done is done. What matters now is not the past but the present. We must salvage the situation, and marry without delay.'

'We must . . . what?' exclaimed Rebecca.

In her astonishment she dug her toes instinctively into the ice and came to a swift halt, leaving Joshua to come to a sharp stop beside her.

'Marry,' said Joshua, turning to face her. 'Without delay.'

'Have you run mad?' asked Rebecca. 'We scarcely know each other, and yet —'

'I can assure you I have never been more sane.'

He spoke sharply, and she was surprised at the harshness of his tone. A moment's reflection, however, told her that he had expected her to fall in with his plans - although knowing her stubborn nature he should have been prepared for her to have her own opinion on the matter - and she realized that her reaction had shocked him.

'I have no more wish to be leg-shackled than you,' he went on, 'but as I have compromised you we must marry as soon as the banns have been read.'

'You have run mad!' said Rebecca.

'You think we should have some pretence of a courtship?' he asked, misunderstanding her. 'Perhaps you are right. If we marry too quickly tongues will be sure to wag, and it's no use our marrying in order to scotch one kind of rumour if all we do is succeed in creating another. We will take our time, then, and have a three-month engagement period. That should be long enough to silence the gossips, and convince them you are not . . . '

'With child?' she asked forthrightly.

He gave a provocative smile. 'I was going to say, enceinte,' he remarked.

'Which is simply society's word for the same condition,' she returned. 'However, you misunderstand me entirely if you think I object to the length of the engagement. I object to the whole idea. I have no intention of marrying you, either with or without a pretence of courtship. I have seen you but three times before today, and even on that short acquaintance I can say that you are the most impossible man I ever met. You cannot seriously expect me to spend the rest of my life with you. I would not —'

'Would not what?' he enquired. 'Save your reputation?'

'My reputation? What, pray, makes you think it needs saving? No one saw us together that night save for George Lacy, and he will not say anything. I will certainly not tell anyone. Will you?' she challenged him.

'No, of course not. But the fact remains —'

'The fact remains that you must have taken leave of your senses. Marry you, indeed!'

'It seems a bad bargain to you?' he asked in surprise.

Looking at him then, with his firm chin and square-cut jaw, his broad shoulders and muscular physique, she had the startling feeling that it might not be such a bad bargain after all.

But what was she thinking? Of course it would be a bad bargain. The whole idea was ridiculous!

'I see no point in continuing with this conversation,' she said aloofly. Then, turning away from him, she began to skate back towards Hetty and Charles. But he caught up with her with a powerful thrust of his firmly-muscled legs and took hold of her round the waist.

To the crowds who skated past them they looked to be skating along in perfect amity, but nothing could be further from the truth.

'Let go of me,' she said.

'No.'

'I demand that you unhand me.'

'We will return to Hetty and Charles together, as we left them,' he said with provoking assurance. 'And we will inform them of our betrothal.'

'You cannot make me marry you,' she said, her voice just as assured as his. She dug in her toes, this time deliberately, until she had come to a stop. She had no intention of returning to Hetty and Charles until this ridiculous nonsense had been brought to an end. 'If you choose to be so foolish as to tell Hetty and Charles that we are betrothed then I will be forced to tell them that we are not.'

Whereupon she skated off. And this time, though his face was thunderous, he let her go.

'Where is Josh?' asked Hetty, as Rebecca skated up to her.

'I . . . wanted to practise a little skating unaided,' said Rebecca. 'He is following me. Ah, here he is now.'

Joshua skated up.

'Well, this has been a most enjoyable afternoon,' said Charles, as the four of them returned their skates to the stall. 'I think, though, if you're ready, it's time for us to leave.' He looked up at the sky. The light was already fading. The short winter day was closing in, and before long it would be dark. 'You'll come back with us to Sloane Street, I hope, Josh? There are some business matters on which I would value your advice.'

Rebecca willed him to refuse. But then she heard him say, 'I'd be delighted.'

Somehow, although she may have won the battle, Rebecca had the feeling she had not won the war. She may have refused him once, but she feared he would not allow the matter to rest. He had a stubborn streak, as she had already discovered. Well, if it came to that, so did she.

They left the frozen Thames and Charles tried to hail a hansom to take them back to Sloane Street. Their own carriage had long since returned home, as it was too cold to keep the horses waiting. But there were few hansoms out and about that day. The weather made the going treacherous, and not all the cab drivers wanted to risk their horses in such conditions. The hansoms which were driving round the streets were therefore in demand, and in the end the party experienced such difficulty in trying to hail a cab they decided to walk back to Sloane Street. Their only proviso was that they would hail a cab if they saw one on the way.

Rebecca endeavoured to walk with Hetty and Charles, but Hetty had already claimed Charles's arm, and it was not possible for all four of them to walk abreast. There was no escape. She was forced to walk behind her aunt and uncle with Joshua. However, she meant to behave with such icy civility that he had no opportunity to raise the subject of marriage again.

She was fortunate, however, as Joshua seemed to have no more inclination to talk than she had.

Doubtless it was because she kept such a brisk pace that they were never out of Hetty's earshot.

At length Hetty and Charles crossed the road. A carriage rolled past behind them, and Rebecca, stopping at the edge of the pavement, glanced to both right and left after it had gone to make sure that all was clear. Some way up the road to their right a solitary rider was heading towards them, but his pace was so slow and his distance from them so great that it seemed safe to cross. Together she and Joshua stepped into the road.

And then, in a matter of seconds, everything changed. The horse was suddenly careering towards them, slipping and sliding on the snow and ice, and bearing down upon them in the most alarming way. Rebecca looked up, and to her horror she saw that, instead of trying to slow the animal down, the rider seemed to be urging it on.

Surely he knows it isn't safe to push the animal to such speed when the road is so slippery? she thought, shocked, as the horse careered towards them.

The rider raised his whip.

It is not the animal's fault, she thought angrily, seeing the man was about to control the horse with cruelty . . . when she had the sudden, alarming feeling, that the whip was not aimed at the horse, but at Joshua. She turned towards him, but he was more concerned for her safety than his own and he pushed her unceremoniously out of the horse's path.

Which left him directly in front of it.

The rider brought down his whip —

'No!' cried Rebecca.

She watched, horrified, as the man's whip hand began to descend, but Joshua, stepping out of the horse's path, reached up to the rider and caught his wrist. There was a brief struggle, and then Joshua wrested the whip from the man's hand.

'What the devil do you think you're doing —?' he began.

But the rider, deprived of his whip, wheeled his horse around. It slipped all over the road before finally managing to find its footing, and the horseman rode away.

'Now what was that all about?' said Joshua under his breath, eyes narrowing; before joining Rebecca on the far side of the road. Turning to her in concern he said, 'Are you all right?'

Rebecca was trying to gather her wits. She could still hardly believe what had happened. The rider had seemed to be deliberately riding towards them and then deliberately aiming the whip at Joshua. But of course that was not possible. He must have been trying to control his horse and, having to wrestle with the slipping animal, had misjudged his aim. Even so it had given her quite a fright.

'Rebecca? Are you all right?' Joshua asked again.

His hands were on her shoulders. His warm, firm touch was reassuring.

It was strange that his hands could be reassuring, she thought inconsequentially. She had never associated Joshua with reassurance. And yet his body was communicating an unmistakeable sense of confidence.

'Yes,' she told him. 'Yes. I'm all right. Just a little shaken, that's all.'

'Fools like that shouldn't be allowed to own a horse,' said Joshua. 'Bringing the animal out in this weather was bad enough, but trying to force it to go at speed was an act of gross stupidity. It's no wonder the animal slipped. Fortunately, no one was hurt. You're not hurt, are you Rebecca?' he queried in concern.

'No.'

'Good. The shock will pass,' he told her gently. 'Still, the sooner we get to Sloane Street the better. You have had a nasty fright.'

'It is nothing, I do assure you.' Already she had collected herself, and was ready to brush off the incident.

'My dear,' said Hetty, hurrying up anxiously with Charles. The two of them, hearing the commotion, had looked round, and when they had seen what was happening they had come rushing back. 'What a dreadful thing to happen. I am beginning to think we were wrong to walk in such treacherous weather. We should have waited for a hansom instead. I thought you were going to be knocked down for sure.'

Rebecca set about reassuring her aunt. 'No. I was never in any danger. It was just an unfortunate accident, that's all. Don't worry, Aunt Hetty; there's no harm done.'

'Fool shouldn't have been out on the roads if he can't control his animal,' said Charles. 'Poor horsemanship if ever I saw it. Wouldn't have happened in my young days. We knew how to handle our cattle back then.'

Exclaiming over the incident they continued on their way, arriving in Sloane Street without further mishap. Even so, Rebecca was glad when they were safely inside.

'You will stay for dinner, Josh?' asked Hetty, when he and Charles joined the ladies after discussing a number of business matters.

He glanced at Rebecca but then, as if realizing there would be no chance of a private conversation that evening - realizing, too, that after her fright Rebecca should not be called upon to discuss anything important - he said, 'Alas, no. I have a number of arrangements to put in hand before I leave London to return north.'

Hetty was not to be put off. 'Tomorrow, then,' she said decidedly.

Joshua hesitated.

Rebecca, suspecting that he had not accepted her refusal, willed him to decline.

But this time he delighted Hetty by saying, 'Thank you, yes. I will look forward to it.'

Rebecca thought, Which is more than I will do!

Chapter Five

Rebecca was reading in the drawing-room. It was the following evening, and she was already dressed for dinner and waiting for Hetty and Charles to come down. Outwardly she was calm. Inwardly it was a different matter. She was under no illusions about Joshua. She knew him to be a stubborn and determined man. There had been a look on his face the day before that had told her he had not accepted her negative answer to his proposal, but she was determined to stand her ground. Marrying Joshua because he had compromised her was unthinkable.

Even so, she fervently hoped that she would not find herself alone with him that evening, so that no possibility of a disturbing and intimate conversation could arise. And really, it was hardly likely, she reassured herself. A small family dinner was exactly the sort of occasion that would offer no chance of anything private. Although an evening at Lady Cranston's and an afternoon at Frost Fair should not have offered an opportunity either . . .

She was rescued from further uncomfortable musings by Hetty bustling into the room.

'Oh, I do hope the food will be hot enough,' said Hetty anxiously. She was every inch the hostess, and was worried about the meal her cook was going to serve. 'It is so difficult to stop it going cold on its journey from the kitchen. In summer it is easy, of course, but in the winter . . . ah well, it cannot be helped.'

'I'm sure it will be perfect,' Rebecca reassured her.

'Well, Mrs Lunn will certainly do her best,' said Hetty dubiously. 'But it is Joshua's first meal with us in over a year, and I would so like everything to go well.'

Then, drawing her mind away from the problems attendant on having guests for dinner she glanced appreciatively at Rebecca, who was looking most becoming. She was wearing a white satin gown *en saque* with a bodice of midnight blue velvet, over which she wore an Indian shawl.

'I am so glad colours have become fashionable again,' said Hetty, her eyes going from the midnight blue of Rebecca's bodice to her own yellow gown. Made of silk, its high waist was ornamented with a gold band, and its sleeves were decorated with gold lace. 'Unrelieved white is all very well, but it never suited me, and I am vain enough to be pleased that colours are now the rage.'

At that moment Charles entered the room, rubbing his hands heartily and remarking that the dinner smelled good.

'Oh, do you think so, Charles? I am so pleased.'

'It will be delicious,' said Charles decidedly.

'Now all we need is Joshua,' said Hetty, glancing out of the small-paned window, across which the curtains had not yet been drawn. 'Oh!' she cried in vexation. 'It is snowing again. I do hope he will be able to get through.'

She need not have worried. The sound of the front door opening and closing could be heard, followed by Canning's deferential tones, and there was Joshua, looking immaculate in a dark tail coat and pair of pantaloons.

He glanced at Rebecca as he walked into the drawing-room, his eyes warming as he saw her, and Rebecca felt her heart skip a beat. Really, it was most unfortunate, the effect he had on her, she thought. Why could he not leave her unmoved, as every other gentleman of her acquaintance did?

'Good to see you, Joshua,' said Charles. 'We were worried you might not get through.'

'It's getting worse,' acknowledged Joshua, glancing out of the window as he took a seat.

'I hope it won't delay you going north?' asked Charles, offering Joshua a drink.

'I hope it will,' countered Hetty, turning to Joshua warmly. 'Then we will be able to keep you in London for a few more weeks.'

Joshua laughed. 'You may have your wish. I certainly can't go at the moment. I've just heard that the roads out of London are impassable. Even the mail has had to be suspended, and if the mail can't get through then nothing else can. But I mean to set out as soon as there is any chance of success. The manager has been left in charge of the mill for some time now, ever since I went abroad, and although I have every faith in him for the short term, I would rather not leave him in charge for too long.'

Charles nodded. 'You must be eager to see the mill again, and take the reins into your own hands. There are some sharp practices going on in some of the mills these days, and it's as well to make sure your manager hasn't fallen prey to temptation.'

'I'm concerned about that myself,' said Rebecca. 'If there are any unreasonable fines being levied, I hope you will make sure they are removed.'

Joshua's eyebrows raised, as though he had not expected her to be so well informed, and she had the satisfaction of having surprised him.

'I have had the good fortune to meet and talk to Mr Cobbett,' she explained.

Joshua put down his glass. 'Have you indeed. William Cobbett's opinions need treating carefully. He has been imprisoned for libel before now, as I am sure you know —'

'His crime was nothing more than speaking the truth,' said Rebecca.

'As he sees it. But he lives in the past. He wants England to return to the days when labourers worked merrily in the fields. Unfortunately, he forgets that labourers did not always work merrily, and that they were often plagued by poor harvests . . . as well as bad backs. Scratching a living from the land can be hazardous. Farmers, as well as mill hands, have been known to starve.'

Rebecca sighed. 'I know he tends to idealize the countryside and I know that he has a dislike, if not to say a hatred, of the mills, but some of his reasons for that hatred are sound. The way spinners are fined a shilling for leaving their window open, for example, or sixpence for leaving their oil can out of place.'

'I agree.'

'And that is not all,' said Rebecca, who had been so convinced that she would have to argue her case that she did not immediately take in what he had said. 'In some mills, men are fined a shilling for whistling.

I warn you, I will not countenance . . . ' Her voice tailed away as his words sank in. 'You . . . agree?' she asked hesitantly.

'Yes. I do. Is that so surprising?'

'Yes. No. I don't know.'

'Just like a woman!' laughed Charles. 'Three answers in one!'

Joshua smiled, but nevertheless he turned to Rebecca curiously. 'Which one is it?'

She frowned. 'Grandfather told me you were ruthless . . .' she began.

'And so I am, in commerce. But not in my dealings with people who depend upon me for their livelihoods. I know what it is to be poor. Your grandfather began life in very difficult circumstances and he told me many stories of those days.'

Rebecca nodded thoughtfully. Her grandfather had told her about the hardships of poverty. 'I knew Grandfather would never have allowed such fines, but as I knew he had not taken an active role in the mill for some time I wondered . . . '

'Whether I would be a slave-driver?' asked Joshua with a lift of his eyebrows.

'Not a slave-driver,' said Rebecca. 'I know that Grandfather would not have left you in charge if you had been that. But a hard taskmaster, perhaps.'

'I am a hard man,' he acknowledged, 'but I am not a monster, as I hope you will soon discover.'

His eyes washed over her disturbingly, and she was pleased when Charles spoke.

'It looks like you two have more in common than you thought,' he remarked.

Rebecca nodded. She had wondered, when she had become aware of Joshua's ruthless streak, just how far this would carry him in his running of the mill, and she had been prepared to stand up to him. But she was pleased to learn that, although he undoubtedly had a ruthless streak - and, in business, she knew, a ruthless streak was necessary - it was tempered by fairness.

Joshua, she was learning, was a man she could respect.

'Still, the mill needs to be profitable,' remarked Charles.

'And I mean it to be.' Joshua took his eyes reluctantly away from Rebecca and gave his attention to Charles. 'But not at the expense of other people's misery. There is no reason why the mill can't be run in a civilised manner and still show a healthy profit.'

'It's a good thing you two see eye to eye,' said Charles, blissfully unaware of the fact that on everything else they were at daggers drawn. 'It doesn't do for partners to be always falling out. It's bad for business. But it seems that my father knew what he was doing when he left you each half of the mill.'

'You don't mind him having left the mill to us?' asked Joshua, looking at Charles.

'Not a bit of it,' said Charles, holding out his hands to warm them in front of the fire. 'In fact, I'm glad he did. I've no head for business.'

'Nonsense, Charles,' said Hetty loyally.

Charles smiled. 'I'm good enough at managing the property my father left me, but I wouldn't have liked to learn about something new. And besides, the mill is so far north it would have been impossible for me to keep an eye on it. An absent owner is never a good idea. As you say, it provides an opportunity for a corrupt manager to operate undetected. No, I didn't want the mill. It would have been a burden to me.'

The door opened and dinner was announced.

Charles gave Rebecca his arm, and Joshua offered his arm to Hetty.

Rebecca breathed a sigh of relief. Thank goodness! The custom that did not allow wives and husbands to go in to dinner together had served her well tonight.

They went through into the dining-room, an elegant high-ceilinged apartment decorated in duck-egg blue. White mouldings adorned the walls, and their brightness was echoed by an Adam fireplace, which was decorated by a line of dancing nymphs. In the grate burned a roaring fire.

Hetty indicated their places, and they took their seats at the long mahogany table. A group of candles were lit in the centre, casting their sparkling light over the glass and silverware. It was a most attractive sight.

Hetty looked a little anxious as the soup was brought in, but the first mouthful showed it to be good and hot and Rebecca saw her relax.

Good! thought Rebecca. At least Hetty will be able to enjoy the evening!

'Do you know,' began Charles, once he had taken the edge off his appetite, 'I think —'

But whatever Charles had been about to say was lost for ever as there was a sudden crash and something came hurtling through the window, narrowly missing Joshua's head. It passed over his left shoulder and landed with a splash in his soup.

'What . . . ?' asked Rebecca, aghast.

She looked at Joshua, relieved to see he had not been hurt. If the stone - for a stone she could now see it to be - had been an inch to the right it would have struck him forcibly on the back of the head.

Joshua, throwing down his napkin, was already striding over to the window and looking out onto the lamplit street.

'Do you see anything?' asked Rebecca, joining him.

But as she looked out of the window she could see as well as he could that the street was empty.

'No. Nothing.' Joshua's voice was grim.

'Oh! How dreadful!' said Hetty. 'Lady Cranston was telling me only last night that her own house had been burgled just before Christmas, and now our house has been attacked. I don't know what is happening to the world these days. It was never like this when I was a girl.'

Behind her, Rebecca heard Charles calling for the footmen as he gathered a party together and went outside in order to search for the miscreants.

And then she felt Joshua put his arm round her shoulder and steer her away from the window. As he did so his arm grazed her skin where, above her long white evening gloves and beneath the short, puffed sleeves of her gown, it was bare. She felt a shiver run up her arm and spread throughout her body. Instinctively she turned to look at him, lips parted, and he, feeling her reaction to his touch, turned towards her, eyes smouldering. There was a look of desire on his face that set her pulses racing. A desire that, alarmingly, was matched by an equally fierce desire of her own.

How had it happened? How had she found herself desiring the most stubborn man she had ever met? The most ruthless and the most perverse? A man who would relegate her to the fireside if she gave him a chance? Who would deny her the right to take an interest in her inheritance? And who, as the final straw, expected her to enter into a loveless marriage for the sake of her reputation? It was of all things the most contrary.

'London grows more dangerous by the day,' sighed Hetty.

Rebecca heard the words through a haze. She could barely hear, let alone think, with Joshua so close by. His presence seemed to be robbing her of an awareness of everything but him: his strongly-moulded features, his mane of hair, his full lips and his penetrating eyes.

With an effort she brought her wandering thoughts back under control.

She could tell that Joshua was making a similar effort. Although his eyes remained locked on hers, he replied to Hetty's remark.

'These things happen,' he said.

He had obviously made an effort to speak lightly, but even so his voice came out huskily. The sound of it made Rebecca feel weak.

Making an effort to control her powerful reactions to Joshua, she wrenched her eyes away from his and fastened them once more on the street outside.

'Do . . . ' She stopped. Her voice was weak and trembling. She tried once more. 'Do you think it will happen again?' This time, her voice came out almost normally, with only the slightest hint of a quaver.

'I hope not,' said Hetty anxiously.

Fortunately, although she had looked at Rebecca sympathetically when Rebecca's voice had trembled, she seemed to think it was nervousness on Rebecca's part because of the stone flying through the window and nothing more.

'But it might,' said Joshua, who was once more in control of himself. Taking care not to touch Rebecca, he guided her back to the table. 'I suggest we stay away from the windows,' he said.

Rebecca nodded. It was a wise precaution, under the circumstances.

Joshua turned his attention to the table. Reaching out his hand he took the stone from his half-eaten bowl of soup. The bowl had been cracked by the force of the stone, and soup was seeping out onto the damask cloth.

'Oh, no!' exclaimed Hetty, suddenly noticing what a mess it was making.

She rang the bell, and a minute or two later she began directing the servants, instructing them to sweep up the broken china and glass, for the table was covered in fragments from the broken window.

'The table will have to be completely cleared,' she told the servants as she superintended their activities.

Joshua turned the stone in his hand, feeling the jagged edges.

Rebecca looked at the stone, then took it out of his hand. She shuddered. It was large and heavy, and the edges were extremely sharp.

Joshua reclaimed it. 'Better not to dwell on it,' he said. 'Come and sit by the fire. You've had a shock.'

'No,' said Rebecca, pulling her shawl more closely around her. 'I must see if Hetty needs any help.'

'No, thank you, my dear, the servants have everything well in hand,' said Hetty. 'Lay the table in the parlour, if you please,' she instructed the servants. 'We will finish our meal in the back of the house. And serve the soup again, if you will. We have hardly had a chance to touch it.'

At that moment Charles walked back into the room.

'Anything?' asked Joshua.

'Nothing,' said Charles, shaking his head. 'Whoever it was has long gone. There was no sign of them.'

'I have ordered the table laid in the parlour,' said Hetty, in an effort to restore an atmosphere of normality. She glanced anxiously at the window. 'I don't feel comfortable eating here any longer.'

'I think that's a wise precaution,' said Charles. 'I don't think we'll have any further problems tonight, though,' he went on. 'Now they know the house is well defended, the miscreants will think twice before attacking it again.'

Rebecca felt her calm returning. It had been an anxious fifteen minutes, but it was over now and no harm done.

Of far greater concern to her was her reaction to Joshua. If he was going to continue to have such a strong effect on her, she hoped he would remove to Manchester as soon as possible. Although even there she would have to see him from time to time, she thought with a shiver, especially as she was determined to take an interest in the mill.

'Come, let's go through to the parlour,' said Hetty. 'Fortunately there is a good fire burning there. We will soon be comfortable again.'

The table was soon re-set and before long they had all settled down to their meal once more. This time there were no unfortunate disturbances, and they could enjoy their mulligatawny soup in peace.

But Rebecca's calm was short-lived. Because once they had finished their main course of ham in Madeira sauce and were about to embark on dessert, Charles said jocularly, 'You don't have any enemies, do you, Josh?'

'Enemies?' asked Joshua.

Superficially the word came out light-heartedly, but Rebecca detected a note of tension in Joshua's voice. A moment later she asked herself how it was that she was able to catch the subtle nuances in his voice. Usually it was something she could only do with people she knew well, but she seemed to be able to do it with Joshua, despite their short acquaintance.

'No, of course not,' Joshua finished.

Again, the words came out lightly, but again there was an underlying tension to them. For some reason, although Charles had enquired about enemies jovially, Rebecca had the feeling that Joshua's thoughts had been running in the same direction.

'Well, of course Joshua doesn't have any enemies,' said Hetty, looking reprovingly at her husband. 'Really, Charles! What a thing to say.'

'Well, it's just that first of all you were almost knocked down by a horse, then you were almost attacked by the rider,' said Charles. He was trying to be light-hearted in an effort to dispel the uncomfortable atmosphere that had settled over them after the stone had been thrown through the window, but he was unfortunately not sensitive enough to realize that he was making matters worse. 'And then, when you came to us for dinner, a stone flew threw the window, missing your head by inches and landing in your soup!'

'Don't be so ridiculous, Charles,' said Hetty sharply.

Joshua smiled, but Rebecca could see that the smile was strained. He was trying to make light of Charles's remarks, but Rebecca had the disturbing feeling that there may be something in them; that Joshua may be in some kind of danger after all; and her thoughts went to the horse that had nearly ridden him down. Had that been an accident, as she had supposed? Or had there been something more sinister behind it?

She did not know. All the same, she could not help feeling anxious.

'No.' Joshua answered Charles in a bantering style. 'I don't have any enemies. But you have no need to worry about your windows. I'll be leaving for Manchester before long and you won't have to worry about any more disturbances with your soup!'

'Well, really,' said Hetty crossly. 'Now, Charles, see what you have done. You have made Joshua feel he is not welcome here. You will always be welcome here, Joshua,' she said, turning towards him. 'You know that. You must come to dinner whenever you want.'

'Of course I know it,' said Joshua kindly. 'Charles was just trying to lighten the situation. And that's the best thing to do with a situation like this; make light of it.' He raised his glass. 'Here's to unbreakable windows!' he said.

Charles, too, raised his glass.

Hetty turned to Rebecca despairingly. 'I do declare, Rebecca, men are just like children. They never take anything seriously.'

Rebecca attempted to smile, but she was ill at ease. She was convinced that Joshua did, in fact, take the matter seriously. Did he have any enemies? she wondered. The idea seemed ridiculous. And yet . . . and yet there had been a couple of incidents. Could they really be nothing more than coincidence?

'And now, if you have finished your fruit, we will retire to the drawing-room and leave the gentlemen to their port,' said Hetty to Rebecca. She turned to her husband. 'But don't be too long. It seems to me you have taken wine enough already.'

And with this unusually caustic remark she led Rebecca out of the room.

The two ladies retired to the drawing-room, where they discussed the latest novels. They had just agreed that Mrs Radcliffe was their favourite writer, and The Italian - the book that Rebecca was engaged in reading - was one of her best books, when Canning brought a message to Hetty to say that one of the parlour maids was hysterical.

'It's the stone,' explained Canning apologetically. 'It's frightened her. Cook's tried to quiet her, and Mrs Yeats, the housekeeper, has had a word with her as well, but after what happened this evening she is convinced the French have finally landed and mean to put an end to us.'

'Oh, dear,' sighed Hetty. 'Ah, well, I suppose it's not to be wondered at. There has been so much speculation about a French invasion ever since the war began that one can hardly blame the girl for being frightened. It is that wretched stone! It has unsettled everyone. All right, Canning, I will come at once.'

'Would you like me to come with you?' asked Rebecca.

'No, my dear. She will probably calm down more quickly if I go alone.'

She left the room, and Rebecca turned her attention to a book of engravings. She was not alone for long, however. Before many minutes had passed Joshua entered the room.

To her surprise - and her consternation - Charles was not with him. He was alone.

She felt suddenly awkward. She stood up and walked over to the pianoforte. There, under pretence of looking through some music, she could keep away from Joshua. For if she drew too close to him, she did not know what her feelings might be. Her fear of being alone with him had intensified, but now it was not because she was afraid of him attempting to persuade her to marry him. Now her concerns were more basic. She was afraid that he might touch her, and that if he did so, no matter how innocent the contact might be, she would melt.

Joshua checked on seeing that she was alone.

'Is Hetty not here?' he asked in surprise.

'No.' Rebecca tried not to sound agitated. 'She has gone to see to one of the parlour maids, who has become hysterical. And Charles? Is he not coming into the drawing-room for coffee?'

'He is taking a tour of the house. He wants to make sure all the windows and doors are properly locked and bolted. After the disturbance this evening it's as well to be certain everything is secure.'

'Very sensible,' said Rebecca.

There was silence.

Rebecca was aware of Joshua's eyes on her. She wished he would take a seat. Then she too could take a seat - well away from him, at the other side of the room.

As if reading her mind he sat down on one of the gilded sofas. He threw one arm along its back.

Rebecca felt a little more comfortable. Even so, she did not relinquish her place by the piano. Taking any seat would put her too close to him.

He did not speak, and as she continued to occupy herself with the sheets of music she felt his eyes running over her in a way that made her feel hot and flustered. She needed to break the silence, and to voice the questions that were circling in her brain.

'Joshua . . .'

'Yes?'

His eyes never left hers, and she picked up a sheet of music, holding it in front of her as though it were a shield, and would protect her - although protect her against what, she did not know.

'About the stone,' she said, clutching the music even more tightly.

'What about it?' he asked.

He stood up and went over to her.

She felt the urge to step backwards. There was a look in his eyes that made her feel strangely afraid.

'It's just that . . . ' Her voice tailed away. She was finding it difficult to concentrate with him standing so near.

He looked at her enquiringly, but with an underlying glance that made her feel more vulnerable than ever.

'It's just that several strange things have happened to you recently,' she said.

'The stone was nothing.' His eyes ran over her face and lingered on her lips.

'Perhaps not.' She took a breath to steady herself, and then continued. 'But it isn't only the stone. There was the horse.'

'The horse was ridden by a fool.'

'I know. But still . . . but still.' Her eyes went to his of their own accord. 'You will take care, won't you?'

He did not speak at once. Then he said, his voice low and husky, 'Why, Rebecca? Does my safety matter to you?'

The words hung in the air between them.

'It does matter to you, doesn't it?' he asked, his eyes searching her own.

She dropped them. For some reason she could not meet his gaze.

'Of course it does,' she said.

'Why?' he asked again.

'Why?' She swallowed, feeling as though she was in a trap.

'Yes. Why does it matter to you, Becky?'

'My . . . my grandfather was very fond of you,' she said, her eyes on the floor.

'And you?' he asked.

'I . . . I would not like anything to happen to you.'

'No?' His voice was huskier than ever.

'No.'

And why did the conversation seem to be so important, when it was about nothing but commonplaces? she asked herself.

'After all, we are partners now,' she said, making an effort to make the conversation seem more normal. But still she did not raise her eyes to his. She was afraid of what she would see there.

'Partners,' he said, his voice low. The word seemed full of hidden meaning. As if sensing it, he added, 'In the mill.'

She could feel his eyes on her, but still could not bring herself to look at him.

'But is that all we are?' he asked.

'Yes. Of course.'

'Then why are you backing away from me?' His voice was soft and sultry.

Her eyes went to his own, drawn there by some irresistible force, as if she could read the answer to his question there. Why had she backed away from him? she wondered. She had not realized she had done so. But he was right. She had taken a step back - only to be stopped by the piano. It was pressing into her, hard and uncomfortable. But she did not move forward again. Because if she did it would bring her closer to Joshua.

'Because . . . ' She gulped.

'Yes?' he asked, his head bending towards hers.

She tried to make some sort of reply but her voice caught in her throat and no sound came out.

'Partners don't back away from each other,' he said, reaching out his hand and lifting her chin.

She had no choice but to meet his gaze. It was so direct that she felt she was looking, not into his eyes, but into his soul.

'Lovers, on the other hand . . . ' he said softly.

She felt her heart fluttering against her rib cage.

'We are not lovers,' she said. She tried to sound bold and confident, but her voice came out in a breathless gasp.

'But we could be . . . when we marry. Marriage has pleasures as well as pains, Rebecca,' he breathed, tilting his head towards hers.

'Marriage!' she exclaimed. And suddenly she was free of the spell that had gripped her. 'Marriage?' she demanded. Her head was held high and her shoulders were flung back. 'So that is what lies behind your behaviour! The desire to seduce me. So that I will agree to marry you!'

'You make it sound like a penance!' he exclaimed angrily, his eyes blazing with copper lights.

'And so it is! To marry a man I don't love, simply because he has some misguided notion about protecting my reputation! It is the worst kind of penance!'

His eyes boiled.

'I have told you before. I will not marry you,' she declared. Her head was thrown back and her chin was high; at that moment she was every inch Jebediah's granddaughter.

'What will it take to make you see sense?' he demanded, his eyes burning now instead of boiling. 'If anyone else finds out we were alone together in my bedroom at *The Queen's Head*—'

'But they will not,' she returned. 'And even if they do, I will still not marry you. I could never marry for those reasons.' Her eyes blazed. 'The idea is unthinkable.'

'Think carefully, Rebecca. This is the last time I will offer you the protection of my name. If you do not accept my hand this time, I will not offer it to you again.'

'Good. Then it will spare me the trouble of refusing it,' she returned. 'Nothing on earth would induce me to accept the hand of a man I do not love.'

'And that is your final word on the matter?' he demanded.

'It is.'

'Then there is no more to be said.'

They stood glaring at each other, like two combatants in a duel instead of two guests at a dinner party.

And then came the sound of footsteps approaching the door on the other side.

They glared at each other for one moment more before sanity reasserted itself and they turned away from each other, both of them trying to regain their composure before Hetty or Charles should enter the room.

Rebecca turned to the pianoforte, where once again she busied herself with the sheets of music. Joshua, striding across to the other side of the room, picked up a decanter and poured himself a drink. So that by the time Hetty entered the room they seemed to be engaging in commonplace activities.

'Such a fuss!' said Hetty, completely oblivious of the hostile encounter that had just taken place in that very room. 'The silly girl was convinced that the French had invaded until I took her to the window and showed her that the streets are empty of soldiers. Ah, well, she has calmed down now.' She looked round, as if noticing for the first time that Charles was missing. 'Where is Charles? Don't tell me he's still sitting over his port?'

'Charles has gone on a tour of the house, checking that all the doors and windows are bolted,' explained Joshua.

'Oh, what a good idea!' said Hetty. 'We don't want any more disturbances tonight. The sooner the war is over the better things will be for all concerned. It is no wonder there is so much unrest, when so many of the people in the country today cannot remember a time when we were not at war with France.'

Rebecca privately though that Hetty was being unduly optimistic in thinking that the end of the war would mean an end of all other disturbances, but she did not say so.

She was glad when, a few minutes later, Charles entered the room and a normal atmosphere was restored. Fortunately, Charles was in a talkative mood, and she did not have to contribute much to the discussion. After her heated conversation with Joshua she felt it would have been beyond her.

Blast the woman! thought Joshua angrily as, back in his own home, he undressed for bed.

Why did she have to be so stubborn? Why couldn't she have accepted his hand? Why couldn't she have let him offer her the protection of his name? Why couldn't she have allowed him to guard her against the wagging tongues of the gossips? Why couldn't she have seen the sense in what he was suggesting?

It was all very well for her to say that Lacy wouldn't talk. That, he believed, was true. But if Lacy had seen them together, then other people could have seen them, too. And the only way to take the wind out of the gossips' sails was for them to wed.

If you think I am going to marry for the ridiculous reasons you propose . . . she had said to him.

Ridiculous? To marry for the sake of her reputation?

It was a down-to-earth reason to wed.

And yet even as a part of him railed at her for refusing him, a part of him admired her. She had not been prepared to compromise her principles, not even for the sake of her reputation.

What strength she had! What determination!

"If only she had been a man!" Jeb's words came back to him.

At the time he had not known what Jeb meant. He knew now. But he could not agree. Because he was grateful, with every fibre of his being, that she was a woman.

A smouldering light glowed in his eyes as he remembered the feelings that had coursed through him earlier in the evening. When she had declared that she would not marry him - when, eyes sparkling and cheeks flushed, she had thrown back her head, her every word, her every gesture speaking defiance - then he had felt a surge of admiration flood through him at the sight of her. He had been filled with the wild desire to sweep her off her feet and carry her to the sofa where he had longed to make passionate love to her . . . .

Oh, yes, he thought, as the image danced before his eyes, he was extremely glad she was a woman. Every inch a woman.

If only she was not such a stubborn one.

He went over to the washstand and threw water over his face and chest.

But one thing was now certain. He must see as little as possible of her. He was powerfully attracted to her, and now that she had refused his hand he must never let himself be carried away again. There could be no repeat of the incident at Lady Cranston's ball. His dealings with Rebecca must be circumspect. He would not compromise Jebediah's granddaughter in any way.

But it was going to be almost impossible to restrain himself.

Chapter Six

Rebecca felt out of sorts. She should have been pleased that she had irrevocably refused Joshua's hand but instead, unaccountably, she felt low in spirits. A week had passed since she had refused him and she had not seen him since. Which was a good thing, she told herself. Because it meant that he had accepted her refusal and did not mean to offer her his hand again.

But for some reason she could not comprehend her spirits were still low.

She picked up her book and wandered over to the window, looking out at the snow. She, Hetty and Charles had spent the last few days enjoying the delights of the winter weather. They had taken a sled into the park and had tobogganed down the slopes - 'I am too old for this,' Hetty had declared, but she had enjoyed it as much as any of them. They had watched a collection of urchins building a snowman, and they had indulged in a game of snowballs. But today it was snowing too heavily to make them want to venture outside.

She was just about to settle down with her book when she saw a familiar figure arriving at the house.

It was Miss Biddulph!

Delighted that her companion had recovered sufficiently to complete the journey to London, Rebecca went out into the hall to welcome her.

She could see at once that Biddy was still weak, and rang for tea whilst settling Biddy by the fire.

'You look tired,' she said sympathetically as she sat down beside Biddy. 'I hope you haven't overtaxed your strength by completing the journey.'

'I am rather tired,' Biddy admitted. 'But I felt well enough to travel, and besides, I did not want to remain another night in an inn.'

'I can understand that,' said Rebecca, thinking of the last night she herself had spent at an inn - although she doubted that Biddy had had a similar experience!

Tea was brought and Rebecca and Hetty, who bustled in as soon as she heard that Miss Biddulph had arrived, set about seeing to Miss Biddulph's comfort; for although Miss Biddulph was acting as Rebecca's companion on this trip, she had been Rebecca's governess in earlier days, and a strong friendship existed between the three of them.

Charles, too, was pleased to discover that Biddy had arrived. Once she had rested he questioned her closely on the condition of the roads, which were now open again after a lessening in the severity of the weather.

'If the mail has got through, then a private coach should be able to get through as well,' said Charles. 'We won't have Joshua with us here in London for much longer, I fear.'

His words proved to be prophetic. That afternoon Joshua called to make his farewells.

'You're leaving us tomorrow, then?' asked Charles, when Joshua had told them of his plans.

'Yes.'

Although she had been expecting it, Rebecca, for some reason, felt her heart sink.

Joshua went on. 'Now the roads are passable there is nothing else to keep me here.'

He glanced at Rebecca as he said it and then looked away again.

The thought crossed Rebecca's mind that, had she accepted his hand, there would have been something to keep him in London: preparations for their wedding.

But of course, she had not.

'It won't be an easy journey, even now,' said Charles, pursing his lips. 'The roads are still very bad in places. Miss Biddulph has been telling us all about it.'

'Even so, I mean to leave first thing in the morning. My work here is done, and I'm eager to take over the running of the mill.'

'We shall miss you,' said Hetty, kissing him on the cheek.

'It's been good of you to put up with me for so long,' Joshua said with a smile.

'Nonsense!' declared Hetty. 'It hasn't been long enough! We have hardly seen anything of you this last week. But you will be in London again before long, I hope?'

'That depends,' said Joshua. 'I will have to see how things go.'

'Well, you know you are always welcome here,' remarked Hetty warmly.

Joshua took his leave of Hetty and then turned to Rebecca. 'Rebecca,' he said, formally taking his leave of her.

'Joshua,' she replied equally formally as he bowed over her hand.

'Your parting will not be of such a long duration,' Hetty remarked innocently, 'for you will be seeing each other again before long.' She smiled artlessly up at Joshua. 'Rebecca will be returning to Cheshire next week, and that of course is very near the mill.'

Rebecca felt Joshua's eyes rove over her face, but there was nothing burning in his glance. Instead, his manner was cool and distant. 'Until we next meet, then,' he said.

And with that he was gone.

The rest of Rebecca's visit passed quickly. She was determined to enjoy herself, and to make the most of her time with Hetty and Charles in the capital.

Miss Biddulph had by now completely recovered from her illness, and Rebecca was glad that Biddy would be able to accompany them on their outings. It was for this reason that Rebecca had asked her old governess to act as her companion on the long journey, knowing that Biddy would enjoy herself in London, visiting the elegant shops and interesting museums, once they arrived.

With the weather a little improved Rebecca, Biddy and Hetty embarked on a number of shopping trips. Cousin Louisa, unable to travel to London herself because of her rheumatism, had given Rebecca a list of commissions, and these commissions Rebecca now set about fulfilling. She enjoyed purchasing the lengths of silk and muslin her cousin had asked for, as well as slippers and bonnets and a host of smaller items that bore the stamp of London instead of the less modish stamp of the provinces.

In this way the final week of Rebecca's visit passed, and before long it was time for her, too, to leave.

'You hardly seem to have been here two minutes,' said Hetty regretfully as she kissed Rebecca goodbye. 'Next time, you must come for longer.'

'If Louisa is fit to travel, I will,' Rebecca promised, returning Hetty's embrace. 'I did not like to leave her too long on her own this time.'

Charles gave her his hand and wished her a safe journey. 'And remember, you are welcome here any time,' he said.

Rebecca thanked her.

Hetty and Charles bade Miss Biddulph farewell, and hoped she would not take cold again from the journey.

Then, fastening the strings of her bonnet and smoothing her travelling cloak, Rebecca pulled on her gloves and the two ladies made ready to depart.

'I have had the squabs warmed with warming pans,' said Hetty, as she accompanied Rebecca and Miss Biddulph out of the front door. 'There are two stone hot water bottles for your feet - one for each of you - and two silver flasks of hot water to warm your hands. The travelling rug has been warmed. I do hope your journey won't be too uncomfortable.'

'It will be better than the journey down to London, I'm sure,' said Rebecca, looking around her. The snow still lingered, but the roads were relatively clear. The worst of the winter weather was over.

'I have had the box of gifts for Louisa put at the back of the coach,' went on Hetty, as she and Rebecca went down the steps, whilst Charles and

Biddy followed on behind. 'I have included one or two little extra presents to make up for the fact that she was not able to come. There is a hamper beneath your seat, and if you get cold, don't hesitate to take a glass of Madeira. It will combat any chills and warm you through until you can reach an inn and spend an hour or two in front of a fire.'

'Dear Hetty,' smiled Rebecca. 'Thank you for everything!'

She stepped into the coach, and once she and Miss Biddulph had seated themselves it pulled away. They waved to Hetty and Charles until the coach turned a corner and then settled themselves down for the long journey north.

It was a week later when Rebecca's coach reached Cheshire. The roads, although passable, had been treacherous in places and the going had been slow. Added to that was the fact that Rebecca and Miss Biddulph had not been able to spend more than six hours in the coach each day because of the cold and the journey had necessarily been long.

The coach's first stop was at Miss Biddulph's modest home. With many thanks - for she had enjoyed her sojourn in London, despite its unhappy beginning - Miss Biddulph climbed out of the coach. One of the footmen carried her trunk to the front door, and Rebecca waited only until he had returned before giving Biddy a final wave and instructing the coach to pull away.

Another hour took her to the gates of her own home, a delightful gentleman's residence in the heart of the Cheshire countryside.

It was three years now since her parents had been killed in a boating accident. During that time a number of eligible gentlemen had offered to take care of her, but Rebecca had resisted them all and had instead invited Cousin Louisa to live with her.

Cousin Louisa, a gentle spinster of straitened means, had been glad to accept the invitation. It was an arrangement which had worked out well for them both. Rebecca's spirited character made up for Louisa's rather timid nature and they enjoyed each other's company. Besides, Rebecca was glad of the respectability Louisa's presence conferred on her, whilst Louisa was grateful to have some companionship.

Rebecca's musings came to an end as the house came in sight. It was an elegant Georgian residence, long and low, with tall windows looking out over the gardens. Welcoming lights streamed out into the gathering gloom of the winter afternoon, and Rebecca felt a surge of happiness wash over her. She was home!

The coach rolled round the turning circle in front of the door. Even before it had stopped Cousin Louisa, wrapped in a large shawl, came out to greet her.

'Rebecca! My dear! I am so glad you are home!'

'So am I!' said Rebecca, giving her older cousin a hug.

'But come, my dear, you must be cold. Let us go in.'

The two ladies went into the house. It was warm and welcoming after the cold and dark of the coach, the familiar cream walls contrasting with the brightly-polished mahogany furniture and the gold of the long drapes.

Rebecca turned to Louisa as she undid the strings of her bonnet and cast her eye over her cousin, hoping that she had not had too much trouble with her rheumatism over the last few weeks.

What she saw did much to reassure her. Louisa was looking younger than her five-and-forty years and her pleasing face, surrounded by soft, mousey hair and dominated by a pair of pince-nez, appeared to be free of pain. Her small, rounded body was held upright, and she seemed to be moving more easily than she had been doing before Rebecca left.

'You look well,' said Rebecca.

'My dear, I feel well! It is those new pills the apothecary has given me! They have removed almost all the pain, and the salve he has prescribed has made my joints move more freely, I am sure. But come into the drawing-room. We must not stand out here talking in the hall.'

They went through into the drawing-room.

Rebecca looked around at the familiar, well-loved room. It was neither grand nor imposing, and the furniture was decidedly shabby, but a warm feeling washed over her as she took off her bonnet. The ormolu clock was still ticking on the mantelpiece, her favourite chair was set by the fire, and the warm tones of the apricot walls gave off a cosy glow. After all the turmoil of her trip to London, it was good to be home.

'Now, sit down and tell me all about it,' said Louisa, her eyes glowing with her pleasure at seeing Rebecca again. 'Or perhaps you would rather go to your room and rest after your long journey?'

Rebecca smiled. Cousin Louisa was obviously eager for news and company, but was thinking of Rebecca in her usual unselfish manner.

'I will just wash, and change my gown,' said Rebecca, feeling a sudden longing to be rid of the dust and grime of the road, 'but then I would like nothing so much as a cup of chocolate and a comfortable cose by the fire.'

'Oh, yes, my dear. That will be just the thing.'

Less than half an hour later Rebecca found herself ushered into her favourite chair and a footstool placed before her feet, and Louisa then settled herself down and looked at her eagerly, waiting for all the news.

'Hetty and Charles send their love,' said Rebecca, sipping at her cup of chocolate, 'and they have sent some presents for you.' She put down her cup and went into the corner of the room, where the box Hetty had given her had been tucked away by Collins the coachman when he had unpacked the coach.

Rebecca picked it up and carried it over to Louisa, putting it down in front of her.

'Oh, how kind!' said Louisa, as she began to open it, unfastening the straps that had been buckled around it to keep it safely closed.

'I managed to carry out all your commissions,' said Rebecca as Louisa threw back the lid. 'I hope you like the things I bought for you.'

On top of the box were the lengths of material Louisa had asked for, consisting of a length of brown woollen cloth, a length of dove grey silk and a length of olive muslin.

'Just the thing,' said Louisa, taking each length of fabric out in turn. 'My old gowns are growing decidedly shabby.' She looked down at the faded gown she was wearing, made of a drab silk. It was rather old-fashioned, and lacked any of the ribbons and flounces that were now *à la mode*. 'It will do me good to have something new to wear.'

And then came various gifts that Louisa had not expected: a Cashmere shawl, a new bonnet and a pair of the softest kid boots, together with half a dozen lace handkerchiefs and a bottle of lavender water.

'Oh, how kind!' said Louisa again, much touched.

There were several more presents in the box, including one of Hetty's cook's excellent fruit cakes and a bottle of Madeira. Then, when the last item had been exclaimed over, Rebecca set down her cup in its porcelain saucer and began to tell Louisa all about her visit to London. She told her about the reading of Jebediah's will, and then told her about the shopping, the visits to the museums, and the afternoon at Frost Fair.

The only things she did not mention were those that affected Joshua. She told Louisa that she had seen him, that he was well and that he sent his love - for he had known Louisa in his childhood as she and her parents had lived with Jebediah for a while. But she said nothing about the uncontrolled horse and the stone that had narrowly missed hitting him when he had been taking dinner at Hetty and Charles's house. Louisa was of a somewhat nervous disposition and the less she had to worry her, the better.

'Freezewater Street!' exclaimed Louisa, as Rebecca told her of the name that had been given to the Thames. And then, as Rebecca told her all about the stalls and booths, the jugglers and the skating, she clasped her hands together and said, 'Oh! I wish I could have been there!'

'As soon as you are well enough to travel, you must pay Hetty and Charles a visit. They would love to have you, and asked me to say so particularly.'

'Oh, my dear! They are so kind. And it does all sound so wonderful.' Louisa gave a sigh. 'I must confess I have been lonely on my own, cooped up here day after day with nothing to do, and the weather so gloomy, and no one to speak to,' she said.

Rebecca put her hand out to Louisa. 'I'm sorry. It was wrong of me to go away and leave you for so long.'

As if realizing that she had made Rebecca feel guilty, when nothing had been further from her mind, Louisa immediately contradicted herself, saying shamelessly, 'Nonsense! You have hardly been gone at all. I have had a wonderful time whilst you have been away. Why, I was only saying to Betsy the other day' - Betsy being the general servant - 'what a nice change it has been to be on my own for a while. Such a tonic for my nerves. I do declare that you did me a very great favour, Rebecca, by going away. And I have had so much to do that I have never been bored for an instant! I have been reading and sewing, and if the weather has been bad outside, why, it has only made me appreciate how snug and cosy I have been inside. And if you do not believe me, you may ask Betsy, for she can vouch for it all.'

Rebecca leaned across and gave Louisa a kiss on the cheek.

'Oh, my dear,' said Louisa, flustered but nevertheless pleased, 'what on earth was that for?'

'Oh, for nothing,' said Rebecca, thinking how lucky she was to have such a lovely cousin. Then, settling herself back in her chair she said, 'Even so, I am sure you would enjoy a holiday, especially as the new pills are doing you good, and I have a suggestion to make.'

She had been thinking it over in the coach on the journey from London and now she had made up her mind. 'As you know, Grandfather left me half of Marsden mill, and I mean to take an active interest in it. I could do so from here, but it would mean a lot of travelling, and with the weather being uncertain that is not a good idea. So I have decided to take a house in Manchester for the next few months.'

'Manchester?' Louisa's face broke into a smile. 'It would be the very thing. There are the shops - not so grand as London, but still, there are some very pretty things to be had along Deansgate and in the Exchange Hall. And then there will be Mrs Emily Camberwell to visit, and her sister, Mrs Camilla Renwick.' Emily and Camilla had been at the same seminary as Louisa in their younger days, and the three had remained friends. 'And of course, best of all, we will be near to our own dear Joshua, who is now in Manchester to take care of the mill! It will be so wonderful to see him again.'

That was the one thing against the idea, to Rebecca's way of thinking, for she was under no illusions as to the strength of her attraction to Joshua and knew that meeting him would be difficult. Nevertheless, as they were partners in the mill it was something that could not be avoided.

'You like the idea?' she asked.

Louisa smiled. 'Of course I do. I think it's a splendid idea.'

'Then it is settled.'

'Emily and Camilla will help us find a house, I am sure,' said Louisa thoughtfully.

'Good. As soon as it can be arranged we will move to town.' She yawned.

'Oh, my dear, you must be tired,' said Louisa sympathetically.

'I am,' Rebecca admitted.

'I will tell Betsy to serve dinner at once. And then you must have an early night.'

Whilst the arrangements for the move to Manchester were being made, Rebecca had time to enjoy being at home again, at least for a short while. The weather continued cold. Fortunately it was not quite as bad as it had been earlier in the year, but still, she and Louisa did not get out much. There was in truth very little for two spinster ladies to do in a modest house in the Cheshire countryside in the middle of winter. The shops and concerts of Manchester, however, would provide a pleasant distraction.

'I hope we have remembered everything,' said Louisa, as at last the carriage was packed and they were off.

'I'm sure we have,' said Rebecca. 'The rented house is furnished, and we have already sent the linen and china up to town with Betsy. And besides, if we have forgotten anything, we can always send Betsy back for it.'

'Yes, my dear, you are right,' said Louisa. 'I am so pleased we have brought a few personal touches with us. They will make the place feel more homely. I am looking forward to hanging Grandfather's portrait in the drawing-room.' She settled herself back against the squabs and stretched her legs out in front of her.

'Have you enough room?' asked Rebecca.

'Plenty,' said Louisa. Her face suddenly lit up. 'Oh, Rebecca, I am so excited! I can't remember the last time I had any fun!'

Rebecca was delighted to see Louisa's enthusiasm. Her cousin had had a dull winter, made worse by problems with her joints, and was in need of some entertainment. Besides, a round of parties and shopping would take Louisa's mind off the aches and pains her pills had not been able to alleviate.

'Then we will make the most of it,' said Rebecca. 'I will have to spend some of my time at the mill, but for the rest of the time we will enjoy ourselves.'

Louisa sighed. 'Jebediah would be pleased. He always loved Manchester. It is where he began his life, and he remained a Northern lad to the end!'

The countryside rolled past the window, with only a small pocket of snow left here and there to show what a hard winter it had been. The grass was green and verdant, and looked as fresh as if it had been new-washed. Above it was a clear, cold sky.

As they drew nearer the city the scenery changed. Meadows and a rushing river gave way to streets and buildings, some fine, others squalid. The recent expansion of the city had brought both good and bad in its wake. Good, because the manufacturing industries had brought work and wealth to the city; bad because it had also brought poverty, for the mill hands could only work when there was work to be had, and in these times of unrest there were often periods of enforced idleness when the war with France or trouble with the Luddites brought mills to a standstill.

But still Rebecca felt her interest quickening. This was where her grandfather had laid the foundations of his fortune, and she felt a connection to the city.

The coach began to move more slowly as the streets became busier. Smart shops now lined the sides of the roads, and fashionable people strolled along the pavements. Gentlemen raised their hats to greet friends or acquaintances. Ladies, followed by footmen balancing columns of hat boxes, disappeared into modiste's. Young children with their nursemaids skipped along, taking some exercise. Brewers' carts rolled past, drawn by plodding cart horses. Hackney carriages went by. And in front of them assorted carts and carriages made their way forward in a bustle of noise and confusion.

'Is it always like this, do you think?' asked Louisa a little fearfully.

'I think it must be,' said Rebecca. 'But I dare say we will soon get used to it.'

'I have not been to Manchester for some time, and I had not realized how much it had grown,' said Louisa.

At last they turned down a broad street and approached the house they had rented for the next six weeks. They had been in the coach for only two hours, as Manchester was no more than fifteen miles from their Cheshire home, but the day was cold and they were glad to arrive.

'Here we are,' said Rebecca, as the coach rolled to a halt.

'We have made good time, then,' said Louisa. 'I was hoping we would be here for lunch, and we are.'

They walked up the steps to the imposing town house and went inside.

'This is lovely,' said Rebecca, looking round with interest.

'Oh, yes it is,' said Louisa as her eyes, too, roved round the hall. 'I am so relieved. It was very good of Emily and Camilla to handle so many of the arrangements. Their brother, Edward, helped too. He is a widower now, and Emily keeps house for him, since her own husband is dead.'

Rebecca and Louisa untied the strings of their bonnets as the coachman unloaded the coach, and they were just about to remove their cloaks when Louisa noticed some cards on the console table.

'Oh, look, Rebecca,' said Louisa delightedly, picking up one of the cards. 'It is from Emily - Mrs Camberwell. And another one from Camilla. And an invitation to one of Emily's soirées, to be held at the start of next week.' Then her face fell.

'Is anything wrong?' asked Rebecca.

'Oh, no, dear. It's just that I thought there might be one from Joshua.'

'He probably does not know we are here,' said Rebecca lightly.

'Yes, he does,' said Louisa, 'for I wrote to him and told him all about it. Still, never mind. I told Emily and Camilla he was here, and no doubt we will meet him at the soirée.'

The house in Manchester soon became a busy one. Louisa's friends, Mrs Emily Camberwell and Mrs Camilla Renwick, were both well known in Manchester, and through their good offices Rebecca and Louisa were quickly made to feel at home. Visitors called, cards were left, and invitations flooded in. Rebecca and Louisa attended a number of dinner parties and other entertainments, but most of all they were looking forward to the soirée.

'Have you decided what you will wear to the soirée?' asked Rebecca. She herself was uncertain as to what she should wear.

'Well, I thought I would wear my new grey silk.'

'The one you had made up with the London material?' asked Rebecca.

'Yes.' She paused. 'I wonder . . . ?'

'Yes?' asked Rebecca, pleased to see the happy gleam in Louisa's eye.

'My long white evening gloves have been darned twice, and I was wondering about a trip to the shops this afternoon.'

'An excellent idea,' said Rebecca. 'I have a few purchases I wish to make as well. I am in need of a new pair of clocked stockings.'

'Oh, yes,' said Louisa approvingly. 'I do so like clocked stockings - though why stockings with embroidery on the ankles should be called clocked stockings I really do not know.' She laughed. 'When I was a little girl I used to think it was because they were decorated with pictures of grandfather clocks!'

'Where shall we go for them, do you think?'

'Emily says the Exchange Hall is the best place for that kind of thing.'

'Then we'll go there after lunch.'

Having settled the afternoon to their satisfaction, the two ladies set out, after a light meal, for the Exchange Hall.

'Mrs Camberwell shares a house with her brother, I think you said?' asked Rebecca as the two ladies climbed into the carriage.

'Yes, my dear. You remember Edward.' Louisa went slightly pink as she spoke.

'No,' said Rebecca, shaking her head. 'I'm not sure I do. I remember Emily and Camilla, but I don't remember Edward.'

'I suppose it is not surprising. I don't think he ever visited with the girls. He is five years older than Emily.' Louisa gave a sudden smile, which took ten years from her face as she remembered the days of her youth. 'And didn't he make the most of it! He used to tease us all shamefully when we were children.'

'You knew him, then?'

'Oh, yes, my dear. I used to see a lot of him in the holidays, when he was not at school. I went to stay with Emily on a number of occasions and Edward was often there. He asked me to dance with him at my very first ball. I felt terribly grown up, even though it was only a private family gathering and I cannot have been more than fourteen.'

They soon arrived at the Exchange Hall, which was home to a colourful bazaar that sold all kinds of interesting and elegant goods. Gloves and stockings, ribbons and purses, all could be bought there, and Rebecca and Louisa spent an interesting hour looking round before finally making their purchases. They were just about to leave the Exchange Hall and venture further afield when they bumped into Mrs Camilla Renwick, accompanied by her husband and by another gentleman.

Rebecca smiled as she recognised Mr and Mrs Renwick. The other gentleman was one Rebecca did not know.

'Well, this is a pleasant surprise,' said Mrs Renwick. 'I had not looked to see you before Emily's soirée this evening. You remember my husband, Henry?'

Henry doffed his hat, and the ladies declared they remembered him very well.

'And this is Mr Willingham.'

Mr Willingham also doffed his hat. He was of middling height with dark brown hair, and was smartly, though unostentatiously dressed. A pair of cream breeches and a blue tailcoat could just be glimpsed beneath his caped greatcoat. On his head he wore a tall hat and he carried a silver-tipped cane.

'Mr Willingham owns a number of mills in Stockport,' said Mrs Renwick; Stockport being a nearby town.

'Really?' said Louisa politely. 'How interesting.'

Rebecca smiled. Louisa had done her best to make it sound as though she really found it interesting, but Louisa was in reality rather appalled by the mills, which could be glimpsed from the coach when the two ladies went out for a drive.

'Indeed,' said Mr Willingham.

'If you are not too busy, why don't you join us?' said Mrs Renwick. 'We are just about to repair to the library for a rest. We can take the weight off our feet, and they also serve splendid ices.'

Rebecca and Louisa happily fell in with this plan, and the five of them turned their steps towards the library. Before long the pavement narrowed and Mr Renwick, who had his wife on one arm and Louisa on the other, went ahead, whilst Rebecca and Mr Willingham walked behind.

'I understand you are Jebediah Marsden's granddaughter,' said Mr Willingham, turning to Rebecca and making polite conversation.

'I am.'

'He was a well-loved figure in Manchester, and is sorely missed.'

'Thank you.'

'You have recently become a mill owner yourself, I hear,' he said, offering her his arm as they crossed a busy street.

'Half a mill owner,' Rebecca corrected him, as they safely reached the other side.

'Ah, yes. Half a mill owner. And which half is it you own?' he asked her.

She laughed. 'I really cannot say.'

'You are to take an interest in it, Mrs Renwick says?'

'Yes. I feel that, as my grandfather left it to me, I should acquaint myself with what goes on there.'

'A laudable attitude. However, if I may issue a word of warning? Although it is a lot easier to be a mill owner today than it was a year ago - the Luddites seem to have accepted that they cannot go around breaking up machinery and times are quieter than they were - there are still outbreaks of unrest from time to time. I hope you won't think it impertinent of me if I ask you to take care. There are those who like the mills, as they bring prosperity to the region, but there are also those who resent the mills for producing goods cheaply and efficiently, and for using machines that take work away from men.'

'Do you think there will be further trouble?' asked Rebecca. She felt she must gather as much information as she could about the situation, and Mr Willingham, being a mill owner himself, seemed to be knowledgeable on the subject.

'That I cannot say. But I believe it would not be wise to rule it out. The ringleaders might have been dealt with, but the name of Ned Ludd lives on.'

Ned Ludd. Rebecca shivered. 'I don't even know who he was, and yet his name inspires fear nonetheless.'

'Reputedly he was a simpleton who lived in Leicestershire,' said Mr Willingham. 'One day, or so the story goes, he broke his stocking frame in anger because he had been punished for some trivial offence. But whether the Luddites really took their name from him, or from King Ludd, one of our ancient rulers, or General Ludd - another name they use to inspire terror - I cannot say.'

'Are there any precautions we can take against attack?' asked Rebecca.

'Alas, very few. A determined man can cause havoc if he wishes to, by breaking into a mill and attacking the machines with hammers, or by setting it on fire.'

Rebecca shivered.

'Forgive me. I should not have mentioned it.'

'No. I'm glad you did.'

'It is not a pleasant thought, particularly for a lady, but forewarned is forearmed. But you have no need to worry about that kind of thing, I am sure. You will have night watchmen at the mill.'

Rebecca frowned. 'I'm not sure. That is something I will have to find out.'

'You have a partner, I understand? He will no doubt see to the mill's security and take care of any difficulties that may arise.'

By this time they had reached the library and Rebecca's conversation with Mr Willingham was brought to an end.

The gentlemen stood back to allow the ladies to enter first and Rebecca was able to free herself from Mr Willingham's company, falling in beside Mrs Renwick instead.

Conversation then became more general. The ladies exclaimed on the wonderful things they had seen in the shops, whilst the gentlemen fetched them ices. Though the weather was cold, the shopping had heated the ladies and they were glad of the cool refreshment. Whilst they ate, they showed each other their purchases, and the gentlemen contented themselves with talking about the war. An hour later, feeling much refreshed, Rebecca and Louisa took their leave.

'For we must get ready for the evening's entertainment,' Louisa said, before she and Rebecca departed.

Rebecca found herself looking forward to the soirée as she stepped out of the carriage later that evening and made her way, beside Louisa, into Mrs Camberwell's house. She was dressed in a becoming gown of white satin with an underskirt of deepest crimson. Deep reds were still fashionable, according to the Ladies' Monthly Museum, and Rebecca was glad of it. Strong colours had always suited her snow-white complexion and her rich, dark hair.

Mrs Camberwell lived with her brother in one of the fashionable new houses that were going up in Manchester all the time. It was similar to the house Rebecca and Louisa had rented, but its furniture and decorations were much more elegant and reflected Mrs Camberwell's fine taste. Gilded mirrors hung on the walls, Buhl furniture graced the living rooms, and Aubusson carpets softened the floors.

'My dears, I am so glad you could come,' said Mrs Camberwell, taking them by the arm and leading them in. 'There are so many people I am longing to introduce you to. My sister, Camilla, you already know,' she said, indicating Mrs Renwick, 'and . . . .'

Rebecca heard no more. Standing at the far side of the room, which had been arranged ready for the evening's music with rows of chairs facing an ornate music stand, was Joshua.

Now that matters had been resolved between them, Rebecca had hoped they could look forward to a normal working relationship. But all such reasonable thoughts flew out of the window when she saw him at the other side of the room.

He was looking more devastatingly attractive than she had ever seen him. His clothes were immaculate, clinging to his body as though they had been formed around him, revealing the hard contours of his broad shoulders and the firm lines of his powerful chest. His hair, by contrast, was rumpled, as though he had run his hands though it. But instead of making him look untidy it made him look vigorous and vital. His face, catching the shadows created by the candles, was sharply contoured, and where his cheekbones caught the light they glowed.

He turned as she walked into the room, but there was nothing burning in his gaze. Instead it was cool.

His apparent indifference hurt her. Despite the fact she had refused his hand she found she could not be indifferent to him. It was not simply because she was attracted to him, it was because of the way she felt in his company - truly alive.

But she must quell such unruly feelings. Because having given her a cold nod he turned his attention back to the young lady he was talking to, and to make things ten times worse, that young lady was Miss Serena Quentin.

Rebecca had met Miss Quentin at a number of the recent dinner parties and she did not like the coquettish blonde, who had a hard, ruthless streak - but then, Rebecca reminded herself, so did Joshua.

Rebecca averted her gaze, but not before she noticed that Joshua was apparently enjoying Miss Quentin's bold sallies.

Rebecca forced herself to give her attention back to Mrs Camberwell.

' . . . Mr Willingham,' finished Mrs Camberwell.

Rebecca managed a polite smile as Mr Willingham bent over her hand.

'We meet again,' he said.

'Yes, indeed,' said Rebecca.

'You have already met?' asked Mrs Camberwell in surprise.

'I had the pleasure of meeting Miss Foster this afternoon, outside the Exchange Hall,' said Mr Willingham. 'I was with Mr and Mrs Renwick,' he explained. 'We repaired to the library and partook of some ices.' He gave his attention back to Rebecca. 'I may be allowed to sit next to you, I hope, when the music begins?'

Rebecca said that he might.

As the musicians set up their music stands he began to tell her all about the excellent concerts that were held in Manchester.

'I wouldn't want you to think the mills are the sum total of the city,' he said. 'We are as cultured as our fellows in London, I hope. Concerts in the Cornmarket are a regular feature of life in Manchester.'

Rebecca answered him politely, but couldn't help her eyes once again drifting to Joshua. Was he really finding Miss Quentin so diverting? she wondered, as he smiled again at something the young lady said.

As Rebecca talked to Mr Willingham about her impressions of Manchester, Mrs Camberwell drew Edward, her brother, aside.

'I want you to pay particular attention to Rebecca this evening, Edward,' she said to him in an undertone.

Edward looked mildly surprised.

'She seems to be getting on very well with Willingham,' he said. 'He's a very wealthy gentleman, and a man of some influence in

Manchester. I thought you would be keen to promote the match.'

'Willingham? Nonsense! Rebecca was made for Joshua.'

Edward glanced at Joshua. 'I hate to contradict you, Emily, but his interests lie in another direction. He seems to be very taken with Miss Quentin.'

'Serena Quentin is a scheming hussy who wants to add him to her list of conquests. But Joshua has too much sense to be taken in by her. He is simply passing the time.'

'He seems to find it a very pleasant way of doing so.'

'Nonsense,' declared Mrs Camberwell. 'Didn't you see the look on his face when Willingham kissed Rebecca's hand? He looked as if he'd like to strangle the man with his bare hands.'

'Really, Emily,' said Edward, but without any hope of changing his sister, or of encouraging her to use less dramatic turns of phrase.

'Which is why I want you to pay attention to her,' said Emily.

'Why?' he asked her innocently. 'So that Joshua can strangle me with his bare hands?'

'Nonsense!' said Emily in exasperation. 'Of course not! So that he'll be jealous, of course.'

'I cannot see the point of making him jealous, when Rebecca, too, is clearly interested elsewhere. She is looking avidly at Mr Willingham,' he protested mildly.

'Only because she has impeccable manners and therefore looks at him when he is talking to her. But the second he looks away from her, her eyes go straight to Joshua. There is evidently some bad blood between them but they are finding it difficult to keep their eyes off each other. See!' she declared triumphantly, as Mr Willingham helped himself to a drink from a tray carried round by a waiter and Rebecca's glance went at once to Joshua. 'What did I tell you!'

Unaware of Mrs Camberwell's well-meaning interference, Rebecca continued to talk politely to Mr Willingham, whilst wishing he would betake himself off to one of the other young ladies who glided round the room. However, he seemed to want nothing better than to stay by her side - as Miss Quentin seemed to want nothing better than to stay by Joshua's side.

Serena was teasing him about something, that much was obvious, and the harder Rebecca tried not to take any notice of it the more the conversation seemed to reach her ears.

'Do let me!' Miss Quentin was saying laughingly, tugging at Joshua's hand. 'It is such a pretty ring, and would look so lovely on my finger.'

Rebecca realized with a sinking feeling that Miss Quentin wanted to try on Joshua's signet ring, the one that had been left to him by her grandfather.

Joshua evidently shared her feelings on the subject, however, for his voice, deep and masculine, carried towards her across the room. 'No.'

Rebecca glanced in his direction and saw him put his hand down firmly by his side. Miss Quentin pouted, but he remained unmoved. 'I will allow no one else to wear that particular ring,' he said.

'Not even your future bride?' asked Miss Quentin, looking up at him with a sideways glance.

Joshua laughed. 'For my future bride I will make an exception,' he said. A moment later dashing her hopes by adding with a sardonic smile, 'But not for you.'

Miss Quentin pouted, but Joshua was impervious to her coquettish ways and making her a mocking bow he left her side.

Rebecca hastily turned her attention back to Mr Willingham, who was exhorting her to choose a seat for the concert.

As the music began, Rebecca thought that the one bright spot of the evening was that Louisa appeared to be having an enjoyable time. The gentle spinster's face glowed and she looked much younger than her five-and-forty years. Edward Sidders had noticed it, too, if the animation of his conversation was anything to go by, and Rebecca was glad. It was time Cousin Louisa had some fun.

Then she gave her attention to the music. The lady harpist's fingers flew over the strings, and the time passed most agreeably until supper

'Ah! Here is Joshua,' said Louisa, as she and Edward joined Rebecca. 'He has come to take you into supper.'

Joshua had not come to do any such thing, of that Rebecca was sure. But Louisa's spontaneous words left him with no alternative and he murmured, 'Delighted.'

Mr Willingham, robbed of his chance to escort Rebecca, made his excuses and then left them, for which Rebecca would have been grateful if it had not meant that she had to go in to supper with Joshua.

She had found his heat and passion difficult to cope with. She was finding his coldness far worse.

'I told Rebecca we would see you here,' said Louisa happily. 'I hoped to see you sooner, but I dare say you have been busy with the mill.'

Joshua responded warmly, and Rebecca was pleased to see that, although his attitude to her was distinctly cool, his manner with Louisa was friendly and unrestrained.

And yet it made her realize that this was yet another feature of his personality which drew her to Joshua - his kindness to those so much weaker than himself.

Her feelings were becoming confused again, she realized. Given that he had offered her his hand for the sake of her reputation she was not sorry she had refused it. But yet the thought of his never offering it to her again made her feel very low.

It was all too difficult. She was not used to such conflicting emotions, and she found them most uncomfortable. But then, wasn't that what love was all about?

Love! What nonsense. In love with Joshua? What an idea! She was perplexed by him. Angered. Confused. Provoked. But in love with him?

Never.

'But come!' said Louisa, rescuing Rebecca from her thoughts. 'We must go into supper, and you can tell us all about it.'

Joshua made Rebecca a stiff bow and offered her his arm. She placed her hand on it, letting her fingertips barely graze it, and they went into supper.

'You must be delighted to be running the mill at last,' said Louisa. 'I know how interested you were in it, and how you spent a great deal of time with Jebediah whilst he taught you all about it. What a long time ago that seems.'

'I am delighted,' Joshua agreed, scarcely looking at Rebecca as he took his place at the table.

'Fancy Jebediah leaving half of the mill to Rebecca! Stocks and bonds, these are what most people would have left, but not Jebediah! He was an eccentric old man, to be sure. But Rebecca has always been so clever, and Jebediah liked clever women. Our grandmother had a keen mind. So I suppose it is no wonder, after all.' She beamed at them both. 'And when are you going to show her round the mill?' she asked.

Rebecca glanced at Joshua. He glanced at her at the same moment and their eyes met. He looked away.

Rebecca had a momentary wish that she had never expressed an interest in the mill; that she had said from the outset that she wanted nothing to do with it; because becoming involved in the mill would mean spending time with Joshua, and despite the fact that she did not love him, she felt a strange connection to him which was making it difficult for her to be in his company.

A moment later she chided herself for cowardice.

Of course she must take an interest in the mill. She owed it to her grandfather. And besides, she was interested, and felt she had a part to play. If she found it difficult to be in Joshua's company, that was simply a misfortune she would have to bear.

'Perhaps we can set a date for my visit to the mill tonight,' she said, as they sat down to a varied selection of appetizing food. 'Now that I am in Manchester I would like to see round it as soon as possible.'

He replied politely but coolly. 'Of course.'

'I thought perhaps Friday,' went on Rebecca. 'If you do not have time to show me round yourself, perhaps the manager can do so,' she said, her courage suddenly faltering.

'Of course Joshua will have time to show you round!' exclaimed Louisa.

'I would be delighted to be of service to you,' he said formally. Though whether he would have said it if not for Louisa's exclamation, Rebecca had no way of knowing. 'Shall we say, two o'clock?'

'Two o'clock,' Rebecca agreed.

She took a sip of wine.

'And I suppose I must go with you as your chaperon,' said Louisa doubtfully.

'You must do no such thing,' said Rebecca. She knew how timid Louisa was, and knew Louisa would not like to visit the mill. 'Betsy will come with me.'

'Well, dear, if you're sure,' said Louisa. She tried to appear unconcerned, but there was a note of relief in her voice.

'Perfectly sure,' said Rebecca reassuringly.

Feeling Joshua's eyes on her she turned just in time to see a hint of warmth in his eyes before he turned away again. He, too, had known how little Louisa would like a visit to the mill, and was pleased Rebecca had spared her the ordeal.

But the warmth was quickly quelled, and later that night, as she readied herself for bed, Rebecca found herself wondering whether it had really been there, or whether she had imagined it.

Miss Serena Quentin's beautiful face wore a scowl as she sat before her dressing table whilst her maid unpinned her hair. The evening had not been a success. Bored of the young men who habitually frequented Manchester's social gatherings she had turned her attention to the harshly attractive Joshua Kelling, only to have him dismiss her as casually as if she had been an elderly dowager, instead of worshipping her as the beautiful and alluring young woman she was. It was bad enough that he had walked away from her - Serena walked away from gentlemen, they never walked away from her - but the fact that he had been seen doing so by Miss Lavinia Madely had made it a hundred times worse.

Serena's scowl deepened as she thought of Lavinia Madely, her only serious challenger for the position of Manchester's greatest beauty. The two had been rivals ever since they had come out. Lavinia's flaxen hair contrasted with the beauty of Serena's guinea-gold curls. Each had their own court of admirers, but Mr Kelling did not seem to want to belong to either set.

"You're losing your touch," Lavinia had smirked when Joshua had walked away from her.

To which she had replied, seriously angry, "I can soon bring him to heel."

Lavinia had lifted one beautifully arched eyebrow. "A wager?" she had asked. "To make it more interesting. Ten guineas declares you cannot bring him to propose."

Fired up by Lavinia's taunting, Serena had accepted. And she had done it with style! "Ten guineas?" she had asked disdainfully. "It's hardly worth my while. Let's make it twenty."

On which sum they had agreed.

Twenty guineas if Mr Kelling proposed.

And humiliation if he did not.

It would have been a rash wager, even for Serena, if not for one thing.

Dismissing her maid she crossed to her escritoire and took out a folder in which she kept her correspondence. Her female correspondence, that was. Her letters from gentlemen were kept in quite a separate place. But her innocent letters, from relatives and the like, were kept in plain view. She took out a recent missive from her cousin and, climbing into bed, read it through again.

The letter had been sent from London, where her cousin Sarah was staying with an aunt. Serena, too, had been invited, but she did not like London out of Season, and so she had refused. But Sarah's letter had made interesting reading. Especially the bit about Lady Cranston's ball.

Serena found the right page and read it through.

You'll never guess who I saw last night, at Lady Cranston's' ball. Mr Kelling! Though what he is doing in London I don't know. I thought he was still in Manchester, running Marsden mill. He is looking more devilishly handsome than ever. But that is not what I want to tell you. Miss Foster is here too! And what do you think? I just happened to be passing the door of the morning-room, quite by chance —

Sneaked out of the ballroom after Mr Kelling, and put her ear to the keyhole more likely, thought Serena spitefully.

— and what do you think I heard? A conversation, revealing Mr Kelling had compromised Miss Foster! I didn't hear all the details, for some clumsy person knocked over a chair and the sound disturbed them —

Really, Sarah, you must be more careful when you are eavesdropping, thought Serena with contempt, realizing at once what must have happened.

— but that is not the end of it, for I happened to see them together at Frost Fair the following day, and as I was skating past —

Sarah is becoming an accomplished spy, thought Serena.

—I accidentally overheard Mr Kelling proposing to her in order to save her reputation. But what do you think? Miss Foster refused him!

Serena scanned the letter again and then folded it thoughtfully, putting it back in her satin folder.

It was this letter which had decided her not only to accept Lavinia's wager, but to double it, for it told her that Joshua Kelling, for all his wild appearance, was in fact a gentleman, and that he would, if he could be manoeuvred into compromising her, propose. That being so she would win her wager and give Lavinia Madely the biggest set-down of her life.

Whether she would actually marry Mr Kelling once she had trapped him into proposing to her Serena did not know. Something about his wildness alarmed her, and she had a feeling that, although she might be able to force him to offer her his hand, she would not be able to control him if they wed.

Still, she did not have to marry him. All she had to do was get him to propose. After that her wager would be won and the betrothal could be broken off at any time.

Putting her letter folder back in her escritoire she climbed back into bed, and with her head full of plans for trapping Mr Kelling she finally fell asleep.

Chapter Seven

'Oh, what an enjoyable evening we had yesterday,' said Louisa the following morning over the breakfast table. 'I don't remember the last time I enjoyed myself so much.'

'You looked to be getting on famously with Mr Sidders,' said Rebecca with a smile.

'Do you know, seeing him again took me right back to my girlhood? For of course I saw quite a lot of him as Emily and I were friends. I had forgotten just what good company he could be. I have been thinking, Rebecca, that we must host an entertainment of our own. Nothing so grand as a soirée, but a small supper party, or perhaps an evening of cards. It will not do for us to go about like this and offer nothing in return.'

Rebecca sipped her hot chocolate thoughtfully. 'Yes, I agree.'

Not only would a small entertainment enable them to repay their friends' hospitality, but making plans would help to take her mind off Joshua, for despite her best intentions she had dreamt of him again last night. Which did not bode well for Friday, and her visit to the mill.

It was with mixed feelings that Rebecca prepared to set out for Marsden mill. Although a part of her was looking forward to learning about her inheritance, another part of her was apprehensive about spending the afternoon with Joshua. His attitude towards her had been distant since leaving London, but there had been moments when she had been uncomfortably aware that he remembered their tense encounters just as clearly as she did. What was more, she had to admit that she missed them, as she missed the fire of his presence and the way he made her feel inside.

However, a cool manner would be much more appropriate this afternoon, and Rebecca determined to be business-like about the mill.

'You will not be lonely whilst I am gone?' she asked Louisa as she put on her bonnet.

'No, my dear,' said Louisa. 'To tell you the truth, I will be pleased to have a day of rest. I have enjoyed our expeditions and our shopping trips, but I am not as young as I was and my joints still trouble me from time to time. Besides,' Louisa added casually, 'Mr Sidders may, perhaps, look in.'

'Edward?' asked Rebecca.

'Yes.' Louisa coloured slightly. 'He has business near here, and he said he might call if he is passing.'

'The very thing,' said Rebecca. 'He will keep you amused whilst I am out without overtaxing your strength.'

The door opened and Betsy came in. 'The carriage is here, Miss Rebecca,' she said.

'Thank you, Betsy,' said Rebecca.

She donned her pelisse, a simple brown kerseymere which she felt would be suitable for the business-like nature of her visit to the mill. Then, taking her place in the carriage with Betsy beside her, she set off.

To begin with, the carriage rolled past the grand houses that had been built in recent years for the mill owners whose fortunes had been made in the city. But as it approached the canal, on whose banks the mill was built, the scene began to change. Run-down buildings sprawled behind the splendid houses of the rich. They were dirty, grimy dwellings, and an unpleasant smell filled the air. Betsy wrinkled her nose, and Rebecca did likewise. But even as she did it she felt a growing determination to make sure that the people who worked for Marsden mill were never subjected to the inhuman conditions of workers in other mills.

Feeling glad she had decided to take an active interest in her inheritance, she stepped out of the carriage when it finally came to a halt beside the gates of the mill. There, right next to it, was the Bridgewater Canal, which linked Manchester to Liverpool. Rebecca remembered her grandfather's pride as he had told her about his choice of site for the mill. "Right next to the canal, Becky," he'd said. "That way we can get all the coal we need quickly and cheaply, and the raw materials, too! Everything comes to us on barges."

Rebecca looked at the canal with interest. She saw the sense of siting the mill next to the canal, and thought with pride of her grandfather's abilities, which had allowed him to take advantage of the new era in manufacturing and rise from being the poor son of a cobbler to being a wealthy and well-respected man.

Then she looked up at the mill itself. It was a large building, and her grandfather had been very proud of its four storeys. Rebecca had to admit she found it ugly but she, too, felt a sense of pride in it, as it was one of her beloved grandfather's greatest achievements. As she looked at the large letters that spelled out the name, MARSDEN MILL, she felt she was a little closer to her grandfather, and she felt a quickening of her interest as to what lay inside.

She was just about to go through the gates when she saw Joshua walking across the mill yard towards her. He seemed very much in charge there, as though he had been the owner of the mill since its beginning instead of for only a few weeks. But then he had been actively involved in the mill during her grandfather's lifetime.

'Well, Rebecca,' he said, after greeting both her and Betsy, 'what do you think of your inheritance?'

'It's much bigger than I expected it to be.' They went through the gates, which were closed behind them by the gatekeeper.

'And uglier?' he asked, lifting one eyebrow.

She laughed. It was no use trying to keep anything from Joshua. Despite their differences he seemed to have an innate understanding of her, and of the way she thought.

'And uglier. But I am still proud of it, and I am looking forward to seeing inside.'

'You should prepare yourself. Cotton mills are hot and noisy places. Come and have a look round.'

She was pleased to find that his manner was welcoming, and she felt on safe ground, knowing that for this afternoon at least they could converse easily on the neutral topic of the mill.

They went into the large building, with Betsy following behind.

'This is the first stage of what goes on here,' said Joshua. He took Rebecca into a long, low room and encouraged her to look round. 'The bales of cotton have to be opened and the impurities removed, ready for carding. Not long ago, it used to be done by hand. The cotton had to be spread out on a mesh and beaten with long sticks to remove the impurities. I can still remember watching the men and women doing it. But now we use a scutcher.'

'What on earth is a scutcher?' asked Rebecca.

'That,' said Joshua, pointing to a large machine, 'is a scutcher.'

The machine looked fearsome to Rebecca. As she watched, she saw how it worked. Men loaded the raw cotton into a spiked drum; the drum spun around very quickly; and a fan blew away the dust and the dirt, the twigs and the impurities, leaving the cotton very clean.

'This is one of the machines the Luddites complain about?' she asked.

'They are usually more interested in breaking looms,' said Joshua, 'but in general they are against any kind of machinery that does the job of a man. I can see their point. But the scutcher does the job of purifying the cotton more quickly and more efficiently than a person, and besides, the job itself is dull, tedious and unpleasant.'

'Bit still, it is a job, and it would pay a salary and allow someone to earn their living,' Rebecca remarked.

'As you say, it would pay a salary and allow someone to earn their living,' said Joshua. 'Although, don't forget, people are needed to load the machine.

Still, there are no easy answers to the problems facing the mills and the workers at the moment. But machinery is the future, Rebecca, and we must go forward if we want to survive.'

'What happens to the cotton next?' Rebecca asked, as they moved on from the scutcher.

'Next it's carded, and then turned into a single thread.'

'Mercy me!' said Betsy. She followed Rebecca and Joshua into an enormously long, low room full of more machinery. 'All this, just to make a bit of cotton material to sew a dress!'

Joshua laughed. 'By the time you buy your fabric at the drapers it's been through any number of different processes,' he agreed.

They moved onwards and upwards, climbing the stairs to the higher storeys. 'Here the cotton is spun,' he said, as they went into another enormously long, low room filled with machinery.

'I never realized it would be so noisy,' said Rebecca, finding it difficult to hear and make herself heard over the clacking of machines.

'You get used to it,' shrugged Joshua.

As if to underline his words, at that moment they walked past a man who was whistling. Although Rebecca found it hard to hear the sound over the noise of the machines, it was clear the man and his fellows were enjoying the tune.

'I'm glad there are no ridiculous fines in our mill,' said Rebecca, remembering that some mills fined men for whistling.

'No. Hill, the manager, is a decent man. He appears to have run the mill very well over the last few months, from what I can see. I haven't had a chance to check everything yet, but so far it all seems to be in good order.' Joshua stood aside to let the two ladies pass back out onto the stairwell in front of him. 'Now that you've seen the mill, I thought you might like to take some refreshment in the office.'

'But we haven't seen the weaving,' said Rebecca.

'We don't do that here,' said Joshua. 'This is a spinning mill. We sell the yarn to other mill owners who do the weaving and dyeing needed to turn it into a finished piece of cloth.'

'Ah! Very well. In that case, some refreshment would be most welcome.'

She smiled at Joshua, and was relieved and pleased to see him smile in reply: a real smile, not one that involved his mouth without his eyes. It seemed that, despite their disagreements, they could be friends - at least when talking about matters relating to their shared inheritance.

The office was a pleasant room, and was less functional than the rest of the mill. Wood panelling lined the walls and a thick carpet covered the floor. Opposite the door a barred window looked out onto the mill yard.

Rebecca looked at Joshua questioningly.

'After all the trouble with the Luddites over the last few years it seemed sensible to take a few precautions,' he said. 'Extra locks were fitted on the doors, and all the windows were barred.'

Rebecca nodded. 'It's unfortunate, but it makes sense.'

Joshua went over to a finely-carved mahogany table that was set within reach of the large, heavy mahogany desk. On it was a silver tray and a variety of bottles and decanters.

'Do you always keep ratafia and seed cake on hand?' asked Rebecca with a humorous quirk of the mouth, as she saw that beside the masculine bottles of spirits, more feminine refreshments had been laid.

Joshua smiled. 'No. There is seldom any call for them. Ladies are not in the habit of visiting the mill. But I'm glad you've come,' he said, handing her a glass of the fruity ratafia, and kindly handing one to Betsy, who was hot and flustered from looking round the mill.

Rebecca was surprised but pleased. It seemed he had accustomed himself to the idea of her taking an interest in the mill.

'I needed to see it for myself,' she said.

She took a sip of ratafia and ate a piece of seed cake.

'Is it what you expected?' Joshua asked.

'I'm not quite sure what I expected, but it is better than I'd feared,' she said thoughtfully.

Joshua sat down behind the desk. 'Your grandfather knew what it was like to be poor, having been poor himself, and he did not let the desire for profit turn him into a monster. There are none of the worse sort of conditions here. The mill is not kept as hot as some of the cotton mills, and there is better ventilation. Water is always on hand for anyone who is thirsty, and children are not taken on too young.'

'However, I'm concerned about their living conditions,' said Rebecca.

'Those are not our concern.'

'Nevertheless, I mean to make them my concern,' said Rebecca.

'I thought you might.'

'You are coming to know me.'

'Yes, I think I am.'

'I know my grandfather was starting to look into ways of providing cheap but clean accommodation for the workers, but old age and infirmity unfortunately prevented him achieving anything. However, I mean to look into it.'

'I can see that your mind is made up. In that case, I will not attempt to stop you. But everything can't be done in a day,' he said, becoming business-like again. 'We will have to take things one step at a time.'

She finished her ratafia and put her glass down on the leather-topped desk.

'And now I must be going,' she said. 'You have given me a lot to think about. But before I do, I have been charged by Louisa to invite you to dinner.'

'And you, Rebecca?' he asked, his eyes looking directly into her own. 'Would you like me to come?'

His question took her aback. She hesitated, but then said simply, 'Yes.' The visit to the mill had dispelled much of the coldness between them and she hoped their present harmony could last.

His face softened.

How melting his eyes are, thought Rebecca.

She wished for a moment that she could have accepted his hand: that it had been offered because he loved her and not because he wanted to protect her reputation.

But what was she thinking? Such thoughts were ridiculous. He did not love her. And she did not love him, she reminded herself.

'I would like to come,' he said, 'but unfortunately I have too much work to do here. I'm still going over the accounts for the last few months. Hill, the manager, seems to be honest and efficient, but I have to be sure.'

Rebecca hid her disappointment. 'Of course. Well, I must not keep you.'

She stood up.

Joshua stood, too. 'I'll see you back to the carriage,' he said.

They walked together back down the stairs to the ground floor, out across the yard and through the gates to the waiting carriage.

Joshua bent and kissed her hand. And then he bid her farewell and she climbed into the carriage, with Betsy close behind her.

Arriving back at the house, Rebecca repaired to her room to tidy herself before joining Louisa in the drawing-room. She started to slip her reticule from her wrist when she discovered it was not there.

'Have you seen my reticule?' Rebecca asked Susan, who was about to help her off with her bonnet.

'Your reticule? Why, no, Miss Rebecca,' said Susan, looking first of all at Rebecca's bare wrist and then casting a glance around the room in case it had slipped off without her noticing.

Rebecca, too, cast her eyes around the room, but to no avail.

'It hasn't got caught up in your pelisse?' asked Susan.

Rebecca removed her pelisse and shook it out. 'No. What a nuisance. Where can it be?' she asked, speaking more to herself than Susan.

'Are you sure you took it with you?' Susan asked practically.

'Positive,' said Rebecca. 'I remember it distinctly.'

She frowned. She could not bear to think she had lost the reticule, particularly as it had originally belonged to her beloved mother.

'Perhaps it slipped from your wrist on your way upstairs,' suggested Susan.

'Perhaps.' Rebecca went out of her room and proceeded to search the staircase. But the search proved fruitless.

'Rebecca . . . Oh! Rebecca!' exclaimed Louisa, startled, as she came out of the drawing-room. 'What are you doing?'

Rebecca gave a sigh. 'It's too vexing. I have lost my reticule and I can't find it anywhere.'

'Oh, my dear, what a nuisance,' said Louisa sympathetically.

'Maybe it fell off in the carriage,' suggested Betsy, who was passing through the hall on her way to the kitchen. But a footman dispatched to search the carriage came back with the news that it was not to be found.

Rebecca was resigned. 'There's nothing for it. I'll have to go back to the mill.'

'But my dear, it's dark,' protested Louisa. 'Why not leave it until tomorrow?'

Rebecca shook her head. 'I don't like to do that. The longer I leave it unlooked-for the less chance I have of finding it. I would hate it to be swept up and thrown out by accident. No, I'll have to go back. It must have slipped from my wrist this afternoon. But don't worry, I won't be long.'

Louisa nodded, resigned to Rebecca's leaving the house again.

Having made up her mind, Rebecca lost no time in dressing herself in her pelisse and bonnet once more. 'I won't be needing you, Betsy,' she said to the elderly maid who had joined in the search. 'I am simply going to the mill and then coming straight back.'

'Of course Miss Rebecca will be needing you, Betsy,' said Louisa, contradicting her. 'You cannot possibly go back to the mill on your own, Rebecca. What would people think? In fact, you had better take Edward - Mr Sidders,' she corrected herself, 'with you as well. I am sure he will not mind.'

'I wouldn't dream of it,' said Rebecca, feeling she had already kept Louisa from her visitor for long enough. However, realizing that Louisa would not let her go unchaperoned, she agreed to take Betsy with her and before long the two of them went out to the carriage again. It had been freshly supplied with stone hot water bottles for their feet, and thick travelling rugs were once again piled on the seat.

Before stepping into the carriage, Rebecca searched the pavement outside the house, but the search proved fruitless. She stepped into the carriage and put her hope in finding her reticule at the mill.

The carriage was soon on its way, and before long it stopped in front of the large building. The step was let down, and Rebecca was about to get out when to her surprise she heard a loud snore coming from the corner of the carriage. Looking round she saw that Betsy was fast asleep! She smiled, then, tucking the travelling rug snugly round the maid and making sure the hot water bottles were nestling against her, she stepped out of the carriage.

'Don't wake her,' she said to Collins, the coachman. 'I will not be long.'

'Just as you say, Miss Rebecca,' said Collins.

Collins began to walk the horses as Rebecca pulled her pelisse tightly around herself, for the day was cold, and went over to the gate. The gatekeeper recognized her and, with a cheery salute, he let her in. She explained her mission, and he promised to search the yard whilst Rebecca herself went inside.

She hurried across the yard, turning the corner of the mill in order to reach the entrance.

As she did so she saw a man some way in front of her, apparently painting the mill wall.

But why would the mill wall need painting, when it was made of brick? she wondered. He could not be renewing the paint on the large white letters that spelt out the name of Marsden mill, as they were on the front of the building and not the side.

She had an uncomfortable feeling that something was wrong. She hesitated, taking in the man by the light of the newly-risen moon. He was of medium height, dressed in ragged clothes, and wore a misshapen hat. One hand was raised in the act of painting and the other was holding the pot of paint.

144

Rebecca was just about to ask him what he was doing, but at that moment he finished his work. He glanced over his shoulder, and there was something so furtive about the movement that Rebecca shrank back. He did not appear to see her - thankfully she was darkly dressed, and was hidden by the shadows - and with a last furtive glance round he loped away from her, disappearing round the far side of the mill.

Rebecca's courage quickly returned and, once she was sure he had gone, she went over to the wall to see what he had been doing. She shivered. In large letters, daubed in red, still-dripping paint, were the words LONG LIVE NED LUDD.

Ned Ludd. Rebecca shivered again as she recognized the name of the supposed leader of the Luddites.

She looked anxiously towards the spot where the ragged man had disappeared. She knew now why she had shivered when she had seen him. On some level of awareness she had known he was up to no good. And she had been right. He must have been one of the Luddites - one of the men who had cast fear into the hearts of the populace in the industrial centres of the Midlands and the North of England over the last few years.

But how had he got in? There was a gateman guarding the only entrance to the mill yard.

One look at the railings that surrounded the mill, however, answered that question for her. Although there was only one way through the gates, any man who was reasonably active could climb over them, and if he chose his spot carefully he could do it out of sight.

Unsettled by the unpleasant incident she continued on her way. She had been planning to leave as soon as she found her reticule but now she knew she must find Joshua and tell him that the mill had been defaced. She could look for her reticule once she had done so.

As she approached the door a new worry assailed her. What if the door should be locked?

But she need not have been concerned. She turned the large handle and it opened. With one look over her shoulder she went into the mill.

In the dark, it did not seem the friendly place it had seemed in the day time. There was no one about and the entrance was only dimly lit. The gas in the wall sconces was turned right down. There was a ghostly stillness, broken only by the distant clack of the machines as they cleaned and carded the cotton.

Summoning her courage, Rebecca began to climb the stairs to the office. She would not feel easy in herself until she had told Joshua about the man with the red paint. Joshua would know what to do, whether they should ignore the incident, or whether they should take it as a warning that the mill may be attacked.

The mere thought of Joshua gave her courage a boost, and she went forward with renewed vigour.

At the top of the second flight of stairs she paused for a moment's rest.

She was just about to go on again when she thought she smelled something. She sniffed. But no. There was nothing.

She began to climb the third flight of stairs, but barely had she reached the top when she caught the scent again, and this time it was strong enough for her to recognize.

Smoke!

It is probably a smell from one of the processes used in spinning the cotton, she told herself, but even as her mind gave her a reasonable explanation for the smell her instincts drove her actions, and picking up the hem of her skirt she began to run up the last flight of stairs.

As she did so she heard a distant thumping noise coming from above.

Her heart began to beat more quickly and she ran fleetly up the last few stairs. As she reached the top the thumping stopped but she could still smell the smoke, more strongly now. She hurried along the corridor, towards the office. She must find Joshua! She opened the office door but by the light of the moon, which was shining in at the window, she could see it was empty. She backed out, turning and wondering what she should do next, and then, to her horror, she caught sight of smoke curling from under the door at the very end of the corridor. A moment later she heard renewed thumping coming from the other side of it and her heart lurched. So that was the meaning of the noise! Someone was shut in!

Running towards the door she grasped the large brass knob and turned it. But to no avail. The door was locked.

Her eyes went to the keyhole.

No key.

'Are you all right?' she called. The thumping had stopped and she wanted to know if whoever was inside was still conscious.

'Rebecca?' came a man's surprised voice.

'Josh!' Rebecca was horrified. 'Are you all right? What's happened?'

'No . . . ' He broke off coughing . . . 'no time for that now. I'm locked in and I can't put out the fire. There's a spare set of . . . ' He coughed again . . . 'keys in the office, in the desk. The top drawer on the left hand side.'

'I'll get them.'

Rebecca flew down the corridor, going into the office and searching for the keys by the light of the moon. The top drawer . . . yes! Clutching the keys she ran back to the locked room and began trying them one by one. Her fingers were clumsy with haste and she dropped them with a clatter.

'Which key?' she asked as she picked them up, fumbling with the large bunch.

'The . . . second . . . largest,' called Josh, between coughing.

Rebecca found the right key by the dim light and put it in the lock. It turned. She twisted the door knob, and Joshua came stumbling out. He was coughing and choking despite the handkerchief he had held to his face and he stopped for a moment, doubled over, gasping in the cleaner air.

Rebecca put her arms protectively round him. She stroked his dark blond hair. It was pure instinct, and as she felt him relax against her she knew that his response was pure instinct, too. There was a deep, intuitive bond between them, that no amount of disagreements could destroy.

But she could not allow herself to prolong the moment, no matter how precious it was. Smoke was billowing out of the doorway and there was no telling how much Joshua had inhaled.

'Come,' she said, closing the door to prevent the fire and smoke spreading. 'We have to get away from here. There's too much smoke.'

The smoke was rapidly filling the corridor. She thought quickly, wondering where it would be best for them to go. Not down the stairs - the smoke was already in the stairwell, and Joshua needed clean air to breath. The office. Its heavy door would have kept out most of the smoke, and there was a window they could open if needed. She guided Joshua, still bent double, into the office, and shut the door behind them. She gave a deep sigh. The air in here was untainted. It would provide them with a brief haven until Joshua caught his breath.

Joshua responded to the clean air. He breathed in deeply, taking the handkerchief away from his face, and was soon able to straighten up.

'I should ask you what you're doing here,' he said, once he had recovered. He took her hands, and there was an unfathomable expression on his face as he looked down into her eyes. 'But there's no time. We have to put out the fire.' He went over to the far corner of the room, still coughing occasionally, and Rebecca saw that he was lifting a large bucket of water which had been standing there. 'I ordered these put here in case of Luddite attacks,' he said in answer to her questioning glance. 'There's one in every room.'

'Then why —?' asked Rebecca, wondering why he had not used the one in the study to put out the fire.

'It had been removed.'

Premeditated, then, thought Rebecca. Up until that moment she had thought the fire had started naturally.

Joshua wet his handkerchief and put it to his face before opening the door. He strode out into the corridor with the bucket of water. Rebecca, gathering her wits, quickly wet her own handkerchief, then holding it to her face she followed him into the corridor.

What could she do? The buckets. Going in and out of the rooms along the corridor she fetched the buckets of water that had been placed there. Joshua stood in the doorway of the study, taking the buckets from her and throwing the water on the flames.

Slowly and surely the water began to douse the fire.

The buckets were soon empty and the fire still burned, but the flames were at long last small enough to be beaten out. Joshua pulled down the curtains and used them to smother the remaining flames, and by the time ten minutes had passed the fire was at last extinguished.

Rebecca sank back against the desk, exhausted. But Joshua seized her by the hand.

'No,' he said. 'You can't rest here. There's still too much smoke.'

He took her hand and led her out of the fire-blackened room and back into the office. They had kept the door closed and the atmosphere was not too unpleasant. He pushed her gently in front of him and then closed the door behind them, leaning back against it in relief.

Rebecca, feeling his strong, firm hand still holding her own, turned . . . and everything changed. She could barely see Joshua in the moonlight, and yet his silhouette, dark and powerful against the black bulk of the door, was redolent of such virile strength that she caught her breath.

How was it that Joshua could make her feel this way? How could his mere presence make her heart race and her mouth go dry? How could he make her feel this sense of breathless anticipation, this time-stopping moment when she longed to be his arms? She wanted to go to him, to feel his arms close about her, to have him kiss her, but she knew she must not do it. She fought against it with all her will, standing there, frozen in the moonlight, whilst every part of her being cried out for him.

And then he pulled her roughly towards him. Catching her round the waist he dragged her close, so close she could feel the firm hardness of his muscular body beneath his clothes.

He took her face in his hands and looked down at her with burning eyes. 'Thank God you're safe.'

She shivered as he pushed a stray strand of hair out of her eyes and she felt a wave of emotion go through her. She was lost in the moment, caring for nothing but Joshua. His hair may be blackened by the smoke and his face may be begrimed but nothing could dim the intensity of his eyes. They looked deep inside her and she began to tremble from head to foot. This was what she had dreamt of; this moment when she swayed against Joshua and felt his arms tighten around her. Her eyes closed and she felt the soft, sweet touch of his mouth as his lips brushed soft, gossamer-light kisses over her face, dropping them with agonizing sweetness first on her forehead, then on her cheek, then on the tip of her nose, her eyelids and her mouth. She felt his hands cradling her face, holding it tenderly yet firmly so that he could kiss her even more deeply, and her arms lifted, her fingers tangling themselves in his mane of hair. And then she was drowning, going under, lost to all else. She surrendered herself to his caresses, and —

She was thrown backwards with a terrible jolt.

Her eyes flew open. And then she realized what was happening.

Someone was opening the door.

It was the rudest of awakenings. One moment she had been in a state of bliss, the next, pushed backwards by the action of the door opening, she was weak and flustered and desperately trying to re-settle her bonnet and smooth her pelisse whilst fighting against her rapid pulse and trying to gather her scattered wits.

'Thank goodness!' exclaimed Mr Hill, the mill manager, as he burst into the room. 'I thought you had been hurt.' He spoke to Joshua, not, for the moment, noticing Rebecca. 'When I saw the smoke I feared the worst. What happened?'

'I think we could do with a little light,' remarked Joshua.

Rebecca marvelled at his voice. He was once more in command of himself, only a slight rapidity of words betraying the fact that he had so recently been in the grip of a strong emotion. No one hearing him now would know that just a moment ago he had been holding her face passionately between his strong hands and kissing her so deeply her whole being had shuddered with the ecstasy of it.

'Of course.' Mr Hill felt his way over to the gas jets that were set into the walls.

Rebecca made the most of the last few seconds of darkness to pull her bonnet firmly back onto her head. She took a deep breath to settle her breathing, because despite her best efforts to calm it, it was ragged and shallow. But by the time the gas was turned up she had regained sufficient composure to meet Mr Hill's surprised gaze with equanimity.

'Miss Foster!' he exclaimed. 'What are you doing here? That is,' he said hastily, as if realizing that it was not his place to question one of the owners of the mill, 'I was not expecting to see you.'

He looked from Rebecca to Joshua in confusion.

'I lost my reticule,' explained Rebecca. 'When I got home I found it was missing and a search of the house and carriage proved in vain. Thinking I must have dropped it whilst looking round the mill this afternoon I returned, only to find smoke filling the corridor and —'

'And to find that she had to help me quench the flames,' interrupted Joshua smoothly.

Rebecca looked at him in some surprise. It was not like Joshua to interrupt her so rudely. But one glance at his bland expression told her that Joshua did not want the mill manager to know the full details of the fire. Why, Rebecca did not know, but he must have a reason for it and so she said no more.

'How did the fire start?' asked Mr Hill.

'That is something we don't yet know,' said Joshua, fixing him with a penetrating glance.

Mr Hill nodded in agreement. 'It will take time to discover the cause. But you are all right, I hope?' he asked, looking from one to the other of them and taking in the full extent of their dishevelment. 'You have not taken any hurt from the flames?'

'Fortunately, no,' said Joshua. 'My study is a mess and will need re-decorating, and it will take me some time to discover if anything of value has been burned, but Miss Foster and I are both perfectly well.'

'That's a relief,' said the manager. 'Still, the fire could have been catastrophic. A lot of important documents are kept in that room.'

'As you say,' replied Joshua.

Rebecca, watching and listening to both men, detected an edge in Joshua's voice. Did he suspect the manager of having started the fire? she wondered. She frowned. Perhaps she should tell Joshua of what she had seen on entering the mill. She looked at him, intending to say something, but stopped short. He was giving her a warning look, and she realized that he did not want her to say any more whilst Mr Hill was present.

'See to things here, will you, Hill?' Joshua asked. 'Check the documents and see if anything of importance has been burned. Then see to the mill. Look for structural damage, have the buckets of water re-filled and make sure nothing is amiss elsewhere. I will be leaving now. I am engaged to take dinner with Miss Foster and her cousin.'

'Of course,' said Mr Hill. 'I'll check everything personally, right away.'

He left the room.

'I thought you couldn't come to dinner,' said Rebecca once his footsteps had died away. She wondered what had caused Joshua to change his mind.

'Had you told Louisa I couldn't come?' he asked.

'No,' she admitted.

'Good. I wouldn't have liked to throw her arrangements out. But I have my reasons for wanting to leave the mill. Reasons which didn't exist this afternoon.'

'And what are they?' asked Rebecca.

'Hill,' said Joshua succinctly.

'Hill?' Rebecca was thoughtful.

Joshua nodded. 'Yes.'

'But why should Hill make you change your plans? What does he have to do with anything?' she added with a frown.

'I don't know. Maybe nothing. Maybe everything. Someone started the fire in my personal office, and I want to know if it was him. I told him just now that I didn't know if any important documents had been burned but it was a lie. I know exactly what has and has not escaped the flames.'

Rebecca quickly grasped his point.

'If it was Hill who started the fire, and if he did it to burn incriminating documents - documents which showed he had been stealing from the mill, for example - then as soon as we have gone he will check to see if they have in fact been burnt,' she said.

'And if they are still intact, he will no doubt avail himself of the opportunity to destroy them,' said Joshua.

'So if any more documents have been burnt in the morning - documents which are perfectly all right at the moment - we will know it is Hill who started the blaze. And we will know why: to hide his own misdeeds.'

'Exactly.'

'But I don't think it was Hill,' she said. She shivered slightly as the scene she had witnessed on arriving at the mill came back to her. 'I don't think he started the fire. I think it was the Luddites.'

The sound of footsteps coming down the corridor alerted them to the fact that they were about to be disturbed as Mr Hill organized a party of men to check the mill.

'We can't stay here,' said Joshua. 'The men are coming to check for fire damage and refill the water buckets. You can tell me why you think the fire was started by Luddites on the way out to the carriage.' He paused. 'You did come in a carriage?' he asked.

'Yes,' she smiled. 'With Betsy. Only Betsy fell asleep on the way!'

He laughed. 'It has been quite a day for Betsy!' He became more serious. 'And for you. Are you sure you are all right?'

'I am.'

'Very well.'

He offered her his arm and they left the study, going along the smoky corridor and down the first flight of stairs.

Rebecca was pleased to be leaving the mill. They could not talk further without being interrupted, and besides, something had occurred to her that did not seem to have occurred to Joshua. Regardless of who had started the fire, whether it had been Mr Hill, Luddites, or some other person, it might not have been important papers they had been trying to destroy.

It might have been Joshua.

Recalling the incidents that had occurred in London - a horse being ridden at Joshua and the rider aiming a whip at his head; the stone being thrown through the window, narrowly missing him and landing in his soup - she felt that if someone really was bent on killing him, he would be safer at Louisa's than at the mill. The thought of which made her keener than ever to leave, and leave quickly.

'Now,' said Joshua, as they reached the bottom of the first flight of stairs. 'Tell me why you think the fire might have been started by Luddites.'

'Because when I arrived I saw a man painting LONG LIVE NED LUDD on the mill wall,' Rebecca said.

Joshua stopped dead. He turned to look at her. 'A man painting the wall?'

She nodded.

He drew in a sharp breath. 'Then it would seem the Luddites are still active.'

Despite his words, Rebecca detected a note of uncertainty in his voice.

'But you are not sure?' she asked.

'The Luddites are well organized and don't attack without reason. They target mills where the wages have been lowered, for example, and not mills like ours. It is possible they have been frustrated by their recent defeats and have changed their ways, but let us just say I am not convinced.'

They went down the next flight of stairs.

As they reached the bottom, Rebecca caught sight of something glittering on the floor - a red spark. Could it be another fire? she wondered with a shock; before realizing it was the beading on her missing reticule. She breathed a sigh of relief. In all the excitement she had almost forgotten about it, but here it was, waiting patiently for her to find it. She bent to retrieve it.

'Your reticule,' said Joshua.

'Yes.' She closed her hand round it gratefully. 'The braiding on the handle has frayed,' she remarked as she examined it. 'It must have fallen off when the braid wore through.'

She put it away in the pocket of her pelisse and together she and Joshua left the mill.

Joshua stopped briefly in the yard to examine the words, LONG LIVE NED LUDD scrawled on the wall. His eyes narrowed as he took in the large red letters, which were still wet and glistening in the moonlight. Then they continued on their way to the carriage.

'Did you get a good look at the man who did it?' asked Joshua as the gatekeeper greeted them, expressing delight that Rebecca had found her reticule.

'Unfortunately, no,' said Rebecca as they passed through the gate.' I couldn't see him clearly. He was just a figure in the moonlight.'

'Then you would not recognize him if you saw him again.'

Rebecca considered. 'I think, actually, I would. Although I did not get a good look at him, he had a curious way of moving. He walked with a loping gait. I wouldn't recognize his features, but I'd recognize the way he walks.'

'Good. That will be useful for identifying him if we ever manage to catch him.'

They approached the carriage, and Rebecca's thoughts turned to Betsy, who had been left outside all this time. Although she had not been in the mill for very long - everything had happened so quickly that it had taken far less time than it had seemed - she was still worried about the elderly maid. But she need not have been. As Collins let down the step and Joshua handed her in she saw that Betsy was still tucked up in the travelling rug. With two stone hot-water bottles at her feet she was snug and warm and still fast asleep.

As Rebecca took her seat, Betsy stirred.

'Why, Miss Rebecca,' she said. 'Are we here already?'

'We are. And ready to go home. I have found my reticule,' said Rebecca.

'That was lucky,' Betsy said, 'finding it so quick and all. I'm glad you didn't have to go into that nasty mill again.'

Rebecca did not enlighten her, or tell her how long she had slept. If Betsy had realized she had been asleep for half an hour, and that Rebecca had gone into the mill without her, she would have been mortified.

'Mr Joshua is returning with us,' said Rebecca as Joshua followed her into the carriage.

'A good idea,' said Betsy comfortably, as Joshua shut the carriage door.

And then they were away, before long arriving at the house, to find Louisa waiting for them.

'I was beginning to get anxious,' she said. She greeted them with relief as they went inside.

'No need,' said Rebecca, smiling reassuringly. 'We are here safe and sound.'

'Did you find your reticule?' asked Louisa.

'I did.' Rebecca held it up to show her. 'It must have slipped from my wrist. Look, the braid has worn through.'

'I thought that must have been what had happened. But never mind, all's well that ends well. And you have brought Joshua with you. I was so hoping he would be able to come. Oh!'

This last exclamation was wrung out of her by the sight of Joshua, dusty and grimy, who was bearing all the signs of having been trapped in the recent fire.

Catching sight of himself in one of the gilded glasses that hung on the wall, Joshua realized that his appearance would need some explaining.

'Unfortunately, I did not have time to wash before I came,' he said. 'Mills can be very dirty places.'

It was not the truth, but Louisa accepted his explanation, and Rebecca was glad that Joshua had spared Louisa any worry, not telling her about the real events of the evening.

'I can quite imagine,' Louisa said. 'You will want water and soap. And towels,' she added, going into hostess mode. 'Betsy, will you see to it that Mr Joshua has everything he needs? Use the guest room,' she said, turning back to Joshua. 'I am so glad you are here. Dirty or not, we are always pleased to see you.'

Betsy, much refreshed after her short sleep, bid Joshua follow her and Rebecca excused herself, saying she, too, would like to wash and change before dinner.

'Of course, dear,' said Louisa approvingly. 'And then, as soon as you are ready, we will eat.'

Chapter Eight

After the excitement of the afternoon Rebecca was glad to be able to relax and eat a superb dinner in the company of her favourite people. She had not forgotten what had happened in London, when a stone had been thrown through the window, but the dining-room in Manchester was at the back of the house and so there was no danger of a repeat of that incident.

Putting all worries aside she gave herself up to an enjoyment of the tasty soup.

To begin with, Betsy had cooked for Rebecca and Louisa, but it had proved too much for her. At their own home in Cheshire she had everything familiar about her, but here in Manchester the kitchen was very different and Betsy was too old to take kindly to change. So, on Mrs Camberwell's advice, Louisa had employed the services of a cook.

'Do I detect Mrs Neville's hand in this?' asked Edward Sidders, as he tasted the soup.

Louisa nodded. 'I'm indebted to Emily for recommending her to me. She really is an excellent cook.'

'She used to work for Emily at one time, but she was tempted away by a baronet,' said Edward with a smile. 'It is only because he has gone overseas that she was once again looking for a place.'

'The baronet's loss is our gain,' said Louisa.

'I have been charged with giving you an invitation to my sister's ball,' said Edward as the next course was brought in.

'A ball. That will be delightful,' said Rebecca.

Mr Sidders turned to Joshua. 'I hope you, too, will be able to attend. It is to be held next Thursday. A small affair - my sister's house has room enough for only ten couples - but even so the evening promises to be an enjoyable one.'

'I'd be delighted,' Joshua said.

Would Joshua ask her for one of the dances? Rebecca wondered. Not knowing whether she wanted him to or not. To dance with him again would be wonderful, but disturbing as well. She had not forgotten the feelings it had aroused in her when she had danced with him in London. But when the ball arrived it would be soon enough to worry about such things.

'And after that we must hold our card party,' said Louisa, as the turbot was served. She turned to Mr Sidders. 'Rebecca and I would like to entertain, even though we are only in Manchester for a short time, and a card party seems to be a simple and yet enjoyable way of doing so.'

'Indeed,' said Edward with a smile.

'You and your sisters, of course, are invited.'

'I'm sure they'll be only too happy to accept.'

'And you will come, Joshua?' she asked him. 'Do say you will. You must not work too hard, you know. You must have some entertainment as well.'

'I would not dream of missing it,' said Joshua with a wry smile.

'Good,' said Louisa, her face expressing her delight. She turned to Edward. 'Now, tell me, where should we go to have our invitations printed?'

A satisfying conversation followed, with the merits of various stationers, caterers and other necessary tradesmen being discussed, so that by the time dinner was over much of the planning for the card party had already taken place.

'Come, Rebecca,' said Louisa, standing up. 'It is time for us to retire to the drawing-room and leave the gentlemen to their port.'

Rebecca stood up and followed Louisa from the room.

The gentlemen were not long in following, and as Edward joined Louisa on the sofa, Joshua joined Rebecca at the pianoforte, where she was playing a country air.

'You play well,' he said.

'I'm lucky to have an instrument here,' she replied as her fingers ran over the keys. 'It came with the house. It gives me a chance to practise.'

She finished the piece, but when she made a move to rise from the stool, Joshua said, 'No. Don't stop. Here.' He opened another piece of music and spread it out on the music stand. 'There are things we need to discuss, Rebecca, and I would rather we weren't overheard. I don't want to worry Louisa, but you were right earlier when you said I don't think the fire at the mill was the work of Luddites. I don't. And until I know who was responsible I would rather you had some protection. It would be too easy for someone to force their way in here if they had evil intentions, and I want you to have some ex-Bow

Street Runners in the house. I know just the men. They're not the best detectives the Runners ever had, but if it comes to it, they'll be able to protect you.'

'I?' asked Rebecca in surprise. 'But I am not in any danger.'

He did not reply, and she said, a little less certainly, 'Am I?'

Joshua's face was unreadable. 'Let's just say, I'd rather not take any chances.'

Rebecca was thoughtful. She did not believe that she was in danger, but she believed that Joshua might be. She decided to share her fears with him.

'I don't think I am the one the attack was aimed at,' she said cautiously. 'After all, I am not the one who has been the victim of a number of suspicious accidents. You were almost run down by a horseman in London, and you were almost struck a forceful blow by a stone coming through the window at Hetty and Charles's house. And now you have been locked in a room that was on fire.' She hesitated. 'I think the fire may have been started in order to try and kill you.' She tried to keep her voice even, but her hands shook and the music came out with an unexpected tremolo.

He looked at her thoughtfully, as if wondering whether agreeing with her would make her worry more. Then, as if deciding that she was too intelligent to be fobbed off with easy reassurances he said, 'It's possible.'

'But why?' she asked. 'There must be some reason for it. And as you don't have any enemies, it must be someone who has something to gain.' Realization dawned on her. 'Your share. Your share of the mill.' She turned towards him. 'Who inherits it, Joshua? Who does it go to in the event of . . . ' She could not bring herself to finish the sentence, and say, in the event of your death.

'No. That is not the answer,' said Joshua, shaking his head.

'I think you are wrong,' said Rebecca resolutely. 'Whoever it is would stand to gain a great deal by your death.'

'I don't think I have anything to fear in that direction,' he said with a wry smile.

The smile took her by surprise. She could see nothing amusing about the situation, and she was determined to make him take the matter seriously.

'Who is it, Josh? Who inherits your share of the mill? Only tell me that and I will tell you the name of the person who is trying to kill you.'

'I don't think so,' said Joshua. 'You see, Rebecca, it is you.'

'Me?' Her eyes flew wide in astonishment.

'Yes.'

'You have left me your half of the mill?'

'I didn't need to. Your grandfather had already taken care of the matter. If I die without an heir, my share reverts to you. It is true, you could make yourself a wealthy woman by murdering me. And you were on the scene very quickly when the office caught fire.' He spoke thoughtfully, as though seriously considering the idea, but there was an unmistakable twitch of humour at the corner of his mouth.

'And I could have invented the story of the dropped reticule,' Rebecca teased him back, joining in with the spirit of his banter.

'But somehow, I don't believe it.' He took her hands, as she had finished playing her country air, and pulled her to her feet so that she stood facing him.

Rebecca's heart missed a beat. She so longed for him to kiss her, but she could tell by his face that he did not mean to do so. And how could he, even if he wanted to, when Louisa and Edward were so close at hand?

And why should she even want him to?

It had felt wonderful when he had kissed her at the mill, that much was true, but she could not allow him to do so again. It was clear he had no feelings for her beyond a certain physical attraction, and under those circumstances she should not want him to touch her again. But to her consternation she realized that she did.

She had wondered, after he had kissed her at the mill and then been interrupted by Hill, the manager, whether he would offer her his hand again. But although he had undoubtedly compromised her, he had not done so. A part of her was relieved, and yet a part of her felt hollow. Because she realized that never, under any circumstances, would he ask her to marry him again.

With difficulty she drew her thoughts back to their conversation. 'Then if I am the person who inherits your share if you die, that is not the answer to the problem,' she said.

They crossed the room and sat down by an elegant console table, on which a book of engravings lay open.

'But who else is there?' she went on. 'Mr Hill, the manager, seems the most likely candidate, and yet he seems like such a nice young man. Still, if he has been falsifying the books . . . '

'Yes,' nodded Joshua. 'If he has been falsifying the books, he would certainly have a motive. He would want to remove me before the discrepancies are discovered.'

'And he was there, at the mill,' said Rebecca.

'He was,' Joshua agreed. 'He is also one of the few people who have a key to the office.'

'A key?'

'Yes. The door to my office was locked from the outside. That means whoever did it must either have taken the key out of the desk in the main office, or used their own key. And the only person with a key of their own is Hill.'

'But anyone could have taken it from the main office?' asked Rebecca.

'Anyone who knew it was there, yes.'

'And how many people know that?'

'Anyone who has worked in the office, and perhaps, anyone who has visited it, but beyond that, no one.'

'Still, it leaves quite a wide field.' Rebecca was thoughtful and then said, 'How did the fire start?'

'I'm not sure.' Joshua shook his head. 'I smelled smoke and went to investigate. When I did so, someone shut and locked the door behind me.'

Rebecca shivered as she thought about what would have happened if she had not, by chance, returned to the mill. 'I don't like it, Josh. I think you need to hire some Runners yourself.'

She turned over a page of engravings, although she was not paying them any attention.

'I intend to,' he said. 'The scrawlings on the mill wall will give me the perfect excuse to hire some watchmen at the mill.'

'And when you are elsewhere?'

'I will hire a few new "footmen", and a "coachman" who are used to dangerous situations. It will not be difficult to take some precautions, with no one else being any the wiser.'

Rebecca nodded. She was still worried, but knew that little more could be done.

Feeling that Louisa and Edward would soon begin to notice if she and Joshua did not join them at their side of the room, she closed the book of engravings.

'Edward and I have just been discussing the arrangement of the card tables,' said Louisa, whose mind was full of the proposed card party, and who had therefore not noticed that Rebecca and Joshua had been deep in conversation.

Rebecca sat down beside her on the sofa and gave her her attention.

'We will have them in here, I think,' said Louisa. 'These houses are not so spacious that we have much choice.'

'Yes, I think they would go well in here,' said Rebecca, gauging the size of the room. 'We could easily fit eight tables in if we arranged the other furniture a little differently.'

'Just what I was thinking. Eight tables,' agreed Louisa. 'That should be plenty.'

'Emily can let you have the card tables, I'm sure,' said Edward. 'She keeps hers in the attics and only brings them down when they are needed.'

'That would make things a lot easier,' said Louisa, thanking him.

The rest of the evening passed pleasantly in conversation, and it was a comfort to Rebecca to know that, however concerned she herself may be about Joshua, Louisa, at least, had been spared any worry.

'What will you wear to the ball?' Louisa asked Rebecca the following morning.

'I haven't decided yet,' said Rebecca, as the two ladies sat at their embroidery.

'I am thinking of having a new ball gown made,' said Louisa diffidently.

Rebecca put down her embroidery. 'What a splendid idea.'

'Do you think so?' Louisa asked, going slightly pink.

'I do. I can't remember the last time you had a new ball gown.'

'Do you know, my dear, neither can I.'

A new thought entered Rebecca's head at the sight of Louisa's pink cheeks. Could it be that Louisa, having renewed her friendship with Edward, was hoping their friendship would develop into something more? Rebecca smiled. She hoped so. She would like nothing better than to see Louisa married to a kindly and intelligent gentleman, and Edward seemed perfect in every way.

'I think you should arrange your hair in a new style, too,' Rebecca said. 'I saw many attractive new ways of dressing hair in London, and any one of them would add a touch of distinction to your new outfit.'

'Well, I don't know, dear,' said Louisa, sounding worried. 'Do you think I should? I have worn my hair like this for so long that I don't know if I would be comfortable having a change.'

'Nothing too drastic,' said Rebecca. 'But if your chignon was a little higher at the back of your head, and if you would let me tease out a few curls around your face, I believe the result would be most becoming.'

'Well, my dear, if you think so, 'said Louisa, going pink again. 'Perhaps it is time I had a change.'

Rebecca went over to her cousin and gently unpinned her hair, then scooped the thick tresses up into a soft chignon, set higher than Louisa was accustomed to wear it. The new height drew attention away from Louisa's rather slack jaw line and focused it on her cheekbones, which were remarkably fine. Deftly, Rebecca pinned the new chignon and then teased out a few curls. The overall effect was softer, more feminine, and undeniably attractive.

'Oh, my!' exclaimed Louisa, as she looked at herself in a gilded looking glass.

'Do you know, I think you should consult a friseur,' said Rebecca, pinning Louisa's hair to hold it in place. 'Your hair is a little long at the front to tease out into satisfactory curls, and —'

'Oh, no, I don't think I could do that,' said Louisa, who found the idea of too much change at once alarming. '

'A pity,' said Rebecca coaxingly. 'I confess I would like to consult one myself, but it seems too extravagant a thing to do just for me.'

'Oh, but you must!' exclaimed Louisa.

'Then it is settled,' said Rebecca, well satisfied with her ruse. 'We will discover the name of the most fashionable friseur in Manchester and go and see him together.'

This notion made it imperative to pay a visit to Mrs Camberwell. It was necessary for the two ladies to discover the names of both a fashionable friseur and a stylish modiste.

By good fortune, the friseur was due to call on Mrs Camberwell the following day, and that amiable lady insisted Rebecca and Louisa should be there to benefit from his ministrations. The business of the modiste was also quickly solved, as Mrs Camberwell called the carriage and whisked the two ladies off to the small but stylish salon that supplied all her clothes.

'Miss Foster and Miss Marsden are both in need of a new ball gown,' said Mrs Camberwell, as the modiste ushered them into the salon. 'The ball is only a week away. Is it possible for you to make their dresses in that time?'

'But of course,' said Madame Dupont. She received a great many commissions from Mrs Camberwell and did not want to lose the custom of so valuable a client. And besides, she always kept a number of partially made gowns to hand for this very kind of emergency.

'Good,' said Mrs Camberwell. 'And what do you have to show us?'

'For Miss Foster, I think the gold silk,' said Madame Dupont. She put her head on one side and surveyed Rebecca thoughtfully. 'It is very fashionable at the moment, particularly when decorated with ribbon or tassels, and 'er dark 'air will set off the colour admirably.'

She clapped her hands, and one of her assistants brought out a collection of tassels, satin ribbons and lace bands.

'With the 'igh waist decorated so,' she said, holding up a lace trimming against the partially-made gold silk gown which had by now been brought out of the workroom, 'and per'aps a twist of ribbon. The sleeves puffed, so, edged with tassels, and round the 'em, the band of lace, so.' She held the trimmings one by one against the plain dress, and Rebecca could see the effect she was aiming for.

'Yes,' said Rebecca. 'I like that, but there are too many kinds of trimming for my taste. I will have tassels round the hem instead of the lace. It will then match the sleeves, and the effect will be less fussy.'

'*Oui*,' nodded Madame Dupont. 'Yes, you are right. Then just a simple twist of ribbon at the waist?' she asked.

Rebecca agreed. The ribbon would give just the right amount of definition to the high waistline.

That being settled, Madame Dupont took Rebecca's measurements and promised to have the gown ready in time for the ball.

'And for Miss Marsden,' said the modiste, her head again on one side, 'I think a shade of orange tawney.'

'Oh, no,' said Louisa, flustered. 'I don't think I could wear anything like that. A nice grey, with perhaps some kind of trim.'

'*Non*,' said Madame Dupont decidedly. 'The grey, it robs you of your colour. You put yourself in my 'ands?' she asked, but in such a way that Louisa did not like to disagree. 'The orange tawney, it will bring out the gold flecks in your eyes and the 'ighlights in your 'air.'

'Highlights?' asked Louisa, bemused. 'But my hair doesn't have any highlights.' She looked at herself in the mirror, trying to see what Madame Dupont was talking about.

'*Mais oui*,' nodded Madame Dupont. 'When the light falls on it, so, it 'as gleams of gold.'

Rebecca glanced at Mrs Camberwell and the two ladies exchanged delighted glances. Madame Dupont had an eye for colour, and had spotted the highlights at once. Moreover, it seemed she was going to be able to persuade Louisa to wear something more interesting than her usual drab colours.

Madame Dupont clapped her hands and one of her assistants brought her a piece of orange tawney silk. When the sample was draped over Louisa's shoulder, even Louisa was delighted. 'Why, I look quite different,' she said.

Rebecca gave her a kiss. 'You'll be the belle of the ball.'

Louisa, flustered, denied it, but when, the following day, Monsieur Toulouse had styled her hair, getting rid of the centre parting she had worn for many years and instead pulling her hair back smoothly over her crown and cutting it at the front so that it was possible to arrange it into fluffy curls, she gasped in amazement as she saw herself in the glass.

'You look beautiful, Louisa,' said Rebecca. She added, 'I am sure Edward will think so, too.'

Emily and Rebecca exchanged glances, then smiled as they realized they had both had the same idea regarding Louisa and Edward.

Rebecca took advantage of Monsieur Toulouse's skill next, with Emily kindly waiting until last. By the time he left, they had all had their hair trimmed and styled in the most becoming way.

'Monsieur Toulouse may not be able to attend us on the day of the ball, but at least we know what we are aiming at,' said Emily as she regarded her hair in the gilded glass.

Well pleased with their morning the ladies parted, and Rebecca and Louisa returned home.

They were just about to get out their workbaskets, after partaking of a delightful luncheon, when there was a knock at the front door.

'I wonder who that can be?' said Louisa, eyebrows raised.

'I have no idea,' said Rebecca. Privately she hoped it was Joshua. It was not impossible that he might call. He had told her he would let her know what had caused the fire when he knew himself, and she had been half expecting him to call all day.

The drawing-room door opened and Betsy announced Mr Willingham.

Rebecca tried to hide her disappointment, and was glad that Mr Willingham turned to Louisa first. It would not be polite of her to let him see she had been hoping for someone else.

Mr Willingham was looking smart and confident. Not for nothing was he one of the most prosperous mill owners in the area. He bowed politely over Louisa's hand before turning and greeting Rebecca.

'Mr Willingham. This is a pleasant surprise,' said Louisa.

'You were good enough to say I might call on you.'

'Of course,' said Louisa. 'Pray, be seated.'

He settled himself in a heavy mahogany chair.

'I have called to issue an invitation,' he said, after they had enquired politely into each other's health. 'My mother is holding a dinner party at the end of next week and she would be honoured if you would attend. I have the card here.' He drew a gilt-edged card out of his pocket. 'It is short notice, I'm afraid, but she feels she must make the most of the opportunity to get to know you, before you leave us again for Cheshire. She is eager to meet you,' he said, turning to Rebecca. 'I have told her so much about you.'

'Oh, the end of next week. How fortunate,' said Louisa, taking the card. 'We have no engagement for that night. Yes, indeed, we would be honoured to attend.'

'My mother will be glad,' he said. 'And so will I.'

'You will be going to Mrs Camberwell's ball, I take it?' asked Louisa.

'Yes, indeed. I am looking forward to it. I hope I may beg the favour of the first dance?' he said to Rebecca.

Finding she had no valid reason for excusing herself, Rebecca was forced to agree to his proposal. But she would rather have given her hand to Joshua, no matter how confused he made her feel.

'Good. We mill-owners, Miss Foster, must stick together,' said Mr Willingham with a smile.

At that moment there was another knock at the outside door and a second visitor was admitted.

'Joshua!' exclaimed Rebecca as she stood up to welcome the new guest.

'Joshua! How delightful to see you,' said Louisa.

'Marsden,' said Mr Willingham coolly.

Joshua nodded. 'Willingham.'

There was a coldness between the two men that Rebecca could not fail to notice. Nevertheless she was glad of it because, when Louisa offered the two gentlemen refreshments, Mr Willingham declined, saying, 'Alas, I cannot stay. I came simply to bring you the invitation. I am delighted to be able to tell my mother that you accept.'

And with that he bowed himself out of the room.

'You will take some refreshment, Joshua?' asked Louisa. 'I was just about to ring for tea.'

'Yes, thank you, I would be delighted.' He settled himself in a Hepplewhite chair.

Louisa went over to the fireplace and pulled the bell. Nothing happened.

'These rented houses,' Louisa said. 'There is always something that isn't working. Never mind, I will go down to the kitchens and tell Mrs Neville myself.'

She had scarcely left the room when Joshua turned to Rebecca and said, 'Invitation?'

'Yes. Mr Willingham's mother has invited us to dine with her at the end of next week.'

Joshua hesitated. 'I would rather you did not go. Willingham's an ambitious man. His family own a weaving mill in Stockport —'

'I know,' said Rebecca. 'You are afraid, perhaps, that he intends to play on my lack of business experience, and you are worried that he will try to secure preferential rates for his family when buying cotton from Marsden mill?'

Joshua laughed. 'The thought had crossed my mind. But I see it had also crossed yours.'

Rebecca smiled. 'I am not my grandfather's granddaughter for nothing,' she remarked.

'No, indeed.' Then Joshua's expression became more serious. 'I may be maligning him, but Willingham seldom does anything without an ulterior motive and all I am saying is that I think it would be better if you were to decline his invitation.'

Rebecca sighed. 'I'm afraid that will be impossible. Louisa has already accepted.'

Joshua frowned. 'That's unfortunate. Still, what's done is done. But be on your guard, Rebecca. If Willingham strays onto the subject of the mill, try and turn him away from it. It isn't just that I think he may try to gain preferential terms from you, I think he may also try to find out details of the running of Marsden mill - what salaries we pay our workers, for example, or how profitable the mill has been in the last year. It would all be useful knowledge for a man who buys his cotton from us. No, I know you would never tell him,' he said, seeing that she was about to declare it, 'but he is skilled at conversation, and may well have the information out of you before you know what you are about. You would not be the first mill owner to fall foul of his devious methods.'

Rebecca nodded. 'I sensed from the moment I met him that he was an ambitious man.'

'But that's enough of Willingham,' said Joshua. 'That isn't why I came here today.'

'You have found out how the fire started?' Rebecca asked.

He nodded. 'Yes.'

Rebecca sat down, and Joshua sat opposite her.

'As I suspected, it was started quite deliberately,' he said. 'A lighted flambeau had been left in the bottom drawer of the desk.'

'To destroy the documents?' asked Rebecca.

'I don't think so,' said Joshua. 'That's what's so puzzling. You see, the documents are kept in a locked cabinet beside the door.'

'So anyone wanting to destroy the documents would have tried to burn the cabinet and not the desk,' said Rebecca slowly.

'Yes. If they knew where the documents were kept.'

'And Hill? Does he know?'

'Yes. He does.'

'Which would seem to rule him out,' said Rebecca thoughtfully. 'Were any additional documents destroyed? When you checked them the morning after the fire?'

'No.'

'Then Hill is not the culprit. It must be someone else. But who?'

At that moment the door opened and Louisa entered the room.

'Tea is on its way,' she said.

Rebecca bit back her frustration. She did not want to abandon her conversation, but now that Louisa had returned it was impossible for her to continue it. She would have to wait until she could have further words with Joshua in private, and who knew when that would be?

Still, there was no help for it. She put her frustration to one side and joined in with Louisa's light-hearted conversation. And Joshua, no less frustrated by their lack of privacy, was forced to do the same.

Chapter Nine

Two new footmen soon found their way into Rebecca and Louisa's house. Fortunately Louisa accepted their appearance at face value, and was too polite to enquire into the origins of the broken nose of one and the cauliflower ear of the other. She was pleased that dear Joshua had sent the men along to add to her consequence and convenience, and expressed herself delighted with their presence

Rebecca was genuinely glad to have them there. So far she had not been threatened in any way, but if the unexplained attacks on Joshua were indeed connected with the mill there may come a time when she herself was in danger, and it was reassuring to have two large ex-Bow Street Runners, disguised as footmen, standing in the hall.

Rebecca was reading in the drawing-room on the afternoon of the ball when Louisa came in looking flustered. 'Oh, my dear, it is too vexing,' she said. 'I have broken my fan. I don't know how it happened. I simply opened it to see if it would go with my new gown, and it snapped in my hand.'

'Never mind,' said Rebecca. 'It's still early. We can go and choose another one. Something that will go with your gown.' She closed her book and set it down.

'It is a nice idea, but my legs are feeling a little stiff, and I fear if I go out this afternoon I may not be able to dance this evening.'

Rebecca understood at once why Louisa was so concerned. Edward had claimed Louisa's hand for the first dance, and that dear lady had spent all week looking forward to it.

'Then I can go on my own,' Rebecca said.

'Oh, no, my dear, you mustn't think of it. You will be wanting to get ready yourself soon.'

'Not for another couple of hours at least,' said Rebecca. 'What kind of fan would you like? A lace one would go well with your dress, I think. Or would you like a painted fan? Or maybe one made out of ostrich feathers?'

'Oh, no! Ostrich feathers would be far too flamboyant! A lace fan would be perfect, it would match the lace trim on my sleeves,' said Louisa. 'But of course it is not important. I can do very well without.'

'I would like a breath of fresh air,' said Rebecca, standing up and stretching. 'I have not been out all day. An hour's shopping will help blow the cobwebs away. I can still be back in plenty of time to dress.'

She had soon donned her outdoor clothes and then she summoned the carriage and was on her way. Accompanied by one of the new, protective footmen she set out for Deansgate, where she meant to purchase the perfect fan to go with Louisa's new gown. There were several shops that sold fashionable items, and she spent a pleasant half-hour browsing in them before selecting a delicate lace fan with ivory sticks.

Feeling pleased with her purchase she returned to the carriage and made herself comfortable for the short journey home. Or at least, it should have been a short journey, but the streets were busy, and to make matters worse a cart had overturned ahead of her, shedding its load of vegetables all over the road. Urchins, drawn by the calamity, were stuffing their pockets with potatoes and carrots, whilst the carter was trying to alternately pick up the produce and shoo them away.

Rebecca watched the scene for a few minutes and then her attention began to wander. As her eyes drifted away from the main thoroughfare and down the narrow streets that led away from it she found herself wondering again about the poor housing that lay behind the fashionable areas. She was determined to provide suitable housing for the workers at Marsden mill, and wondered whether any of the run-down buildings she could just glimpse might be suitable for renovation.

As her eyes began to adjust to the gloomier conditions that prevailed beyond the main street she began to make out more detail: houses, pavements - and then something caught her attention and she sat up straight. There! Loping down the dingy back street was the man who had daubed the Luddite slogan on the wall of the mill!

There could be no mistake.

Deciding quickly on a course of action, she opened the carriage door and jumped out, calling to the footman as she did so, 'Follow me!'

Once free of the carriage she hurried down the narrow street, following the man with the loping gait. He turned down a cross street and Rebecca followed. The street was narrow, and when he turned again it was into an even narrower one.

The houses crowded in on her but Rebecca did not give up. If she could apprehend the man she could discover why he had painted the slogan on the wall. And if he had been paid to do it, she could discover who had paid him.

She saw him hesitate outside a mean house and then he went in. She turned round to signal to the footman, only to find he was not there.

He had been following her when she left the carriage, she had made certain of it, but now he was nowhere in sight. He must have lost her after one of her many twists and turns.

She crept closer to the house, pressing herself against the wall next to the window, determined to learn anything she could, when suddenly the door opened again and the furtive man came out.

'What the 'ell are you doing?' he demanded, his foxy eyes boring into her.

Lifting her chin, she brazened it out.

'I am looking for the Exchange Hall,' she said resolutely. 'You will give me directions, if you please.'

As she spoke she took in details of the man's appearance, in case she had to identify him at some future date. He was short, only an inch or two taller than she was herself, which put him at about five foot six. He had dark, lank hair and long side whiskers. His eyes were small and set close together. His lips were thin and his chin was pointed. His body, too, was thin and wiry. Though small, she guessed he would possess a great deal of strength.

'Lost your way, did you?' he sneered. 'Looking for the Exchange 'all?' His tone was menacing. 'Pull the other one, it's got bells on.' Then his eyes became sharper and he stood up straight. ''ere, 'aven't I seen you somewhere before?'

'I very much doubt it,' she said, giving him a quelling glance.

'I know where I've seen you before,' he said, as realization dawned on him. 'You were at the mill. Thought I didn't see you, didn't you? Slinking back into the shadows. Well you were wrong.'

His hand whipped out and caught her arm. His grip was like iron and his fingers bit into her, even through her cloak. Then, opening the door behind him he tried to drag her into the house.

Rebecca wrested herself free and kicked him hard on the shin before turning to run, but he caught her arm again and said menacingly, 'You'll pay for that.'

He raised his hand to her and Rebecca lifted her arm to shield herself - and then, before she knew what was happening, someone was standing in front of her and blocking the man's blow.

Joshua! But what was he doing here?

Regardless, she was very glad to see him.

He caught the fist that was aiming at his head, then deflected a second blow which was aimed at his mid-section. With a few moves he defended himself and then turned the tables on his assailant, just as the footman ran up.

'Where have you been?' demanded Joshua, glaring at the footman. 'You were supposed to be protecting Miss Foster. Where were you when she needed you?'

'I lost her —' began the footman.

'Call yourself a Runner?' asked Joshua fiercely. 'A blind beggar could have made a better job of protecting her than you've done. What am I paying you for, man?'

'A Bow Street Runner?' asked the wiry man, his small eyes darting from one to the other of his captors.

'That's right,' said Joshua. 'A Bow Street Runner. And one who can testify to the fact you attacked a young lady.'

'Lady?' sneered the wiry man. 'If she's a lady, what's she doing creeping around the back streets of Manchester on her own. Doesn't seem very ladylike to me.'

Joshua tightened his grip on the man. 'I suggest you keep a civil tongue in your head,' he said.

'Oh! So that's the way it is, is it? Sweet on 'er, are you? I wouldn't mind a bit of that myself —'

'Take him in charge,' said Joshua, ignoring the man's taunts and pushing him towards the footman. 'He is guilty of attacking Miss Foster. And don't let him get away.'

'Oh, I won't let him get away,' said the footman, looking at the wiry man with a crooked smile. 'I've got a bone or two to pick with him.'

Rebecca and Joshua looked at the footman curiously.

'Do you know him?' Joshua asked.

'Oh, yes. He's known to us, is Cyril Dunn,' said the footman.

''Ow do you know my name?' asked the man who had just been identified as Cyril Dunn.

The footman removed his powdered wig.

Dunn's face fell. 'Well, I'll be . . . Odgers,' he said, going white.

'Yes, my lad. Odgers,' said the footman with relish. Then he turned to Joshua. 'This cove's wanted for any number of things. He'll do any amount of dirty work, so long as he's well paid. We'd have got to him sooner or later.'

'It's a pity it wasn't sooner,' remarked Joshua.

The footman looked abashed. 'But if I'm meant to look after Dunn, who's going to look after Miss Foster?' he said, in an effort to make amends for losing her earlier.

'Miss Foster,' said Joshua curtly, 'is coming with me.'

Rebecca opened her mouth to speak but in fact she would be very glad to leave the maze of narrow streets behind. She could tell he was angry but their argument could wait until they were somewhere more respectable.

They walked in frosty silence, traversing the maze of dark streets and then emerging into a more respectable area, where they arrived at an impressive residence.

'Thank you for your assistance,' said Rebecca. 'I believe I can find my own way from here.'

'Your carriage has gone on without you,' he said. 'You can wait inside. This is my house.'

'I can't go in without a chaperon,' Rebecca remarked.

'Indeed you can,' he said.

She knew how difficult it would be to find a hansom and so she preceded him into the house.

He waved away the lackeys who would otherwise have greeted him and guided Rebecca through into the sitting-room. It was furnished in a simple and masculine style. There were no floral curtains or cushions scattered around. Everything was of good quality, but plain.

'Now, why don't you tell me what you were doing, putting yourself in danger like that,' he said, glaring at her as he closed the door.

'Thank you,' retorted Rebecca, annoyed by his high-handed attitude. 'I would like some refreshment. How kind of you to offer it.'

She glared right back at him.

'What were you doing in the back streets of Manchester on your own?' demanded Joshua, ignoring her remarks and going straight to the heart of the matter.

'I might well ask you the same question,' she returned.

'I was looking at a number of properties. There are some houses there for sale at a reasonable price, and although squalid at the moment they could be made clean and comfortable for the mill workers. I was going to tell you about them later, and ask if you thought we should invest in them.'

'Ah! I see,' said Rebecca.

'I have answered your question, now you answer mine. You know how dangerous the back streets are, Rebecca, you are not a fool. Even in ordinary times it is dangerous to go too far from the main streets, and when there has already been an unexplained attack on the mill it is madness.'

'I didn't go into the back streets on my own,' returned Rebecca. 'I went with one of the footmen you gave me.'

'If that's the case, then how is it he wasn't with you when I found you?' he demanded.

'Because he couldn't keep up with me. I had to leave the carriage in a hurry,' she explained. 'It was stuck behind an overturned cart, and as I passed the time by looking out of the windows I saw a man I recognized loping through the back streets. It was the man who daubed LONG LIVE NED LUDD on the wall at the mill.'

Joshua's eyebrows shot up.

'I assumed he was just a common thug intent on stealing your reticule,' he said. 'But now I begin to understand. Are you sure? You didn't get a good look at him, and you can only have seen him from a distance when you were in the carriage.'

'I am. It wasn't his looks I recognized, but the way he moved. He has a curious loping gait, as I told you at the time. I jumped out of the carriage in order to follow him and called to the footman to accompany me. I looked over my shoulder to make sure he had done so, but he must have lost me shortly afterwards. I had to keep Dunn in sight, and it entailed making a number of quick turns.'

Joshua's face relaxed.

'So you see, I wasn't putting myself in danger,' explained Rebecca.

'Of course you were,' said Joshua, not so easily mollified. 'As soon as you got out of the carriage you were in danger. And when I think of you following a man you knew to be a criminal . . . ' His face darkened and his eyes became turbulent.

'How else was I going to catch him?' she demanded. 'At least now we have something to go on. As soon as we've questioned him —'

'We?'

'You seem to forget that I'm involved in this just as much as you are,' she returned.

'No. I don't forget. But if you think I'm going to let you anywhere near a man like that you're mistaken,' he said.

'It isn't up to you to tell me what to do,' she returned.

He glared at her. Then said, apparently reasonably, 'You're right. It isn't.' His reasonableness suddenly vanished. 'But I'm going to do it anyway.'

Rebecca gave a sigh. It was no use arguing with him. He could be extremely stubborn when he chose – as stubborn as she was. Besides, she had to admit, if only to herself, that she was actually relieved. She did not relish the idea of seeing any more of Dunn than she had to.

'Very well.'

His eyebrows lifted in surprise. Then he said, with a disarming smile, 'Thank you.'

'For what?' She was surprised.

'For letting me have my own way.'

She smiled, too. 'As long as you don't have it too often, I can't see that it will do you any harm!' she teased him.

He laughed.

'Then for once we are in agreement. And luckily so, for there is no saying who would win otherwise! But now that we have sorted that out, let me offer you some refreshments. You're right, I should have done so straight away. You must be cold and tired.'

'Thank you, but I can't stay. I have already been longer than I intended to be, and I don't want Louisa to worry. I only went out to buy her a fan,' she explained. 'I should have been back by now. I dread to think what has happened to my carriage.'

'Don't worry. I sent Odgers to find it.'

'But —'

'Dunn is being safely held in the kitchen by a couple of Odgers's colleagues - men who, incidentally, will not let Odgers forget that he lost his charge,' said Joshua with a wry smile.

'It wasn't his fault,' said Rebecca.

'Yes, it was. He was employed to look after you and he failed. But if you want to make his life easier in future, don't go jumping out of any more carriages!'

'I'll try not to,' she returned with a lift at the corner of her mouth. Then she became more serious. 'You will let me know, Joshua? What you find out?'

'Of course. You're going to the ball tonight?'

'Yes. Louisa and I will both be there.'

'Meet me in the library at twelve o'clock. The ball should be in full swing by then and no one will notice if we absent ourselves for a while. Then I can tell you what I have discovered.'

'What do you think? Now?'

Joshua ran his hand through his thick hair. 'I think Dunn will be able to tell us very little. He was probably paid to paint a Luddite slogan on the wall of the mill, but I will be surprised if he can tell us who paid him. He was most probably approached in a tavern and offered money to do it, no questions asked.'

Rebecca nodded. It seemed only too likely.

'But I'll have him followed - when I let him go,' said Joshua.

'You're not going to hand him over to the authorities, then?' asked Rebecca in surprise.

'No. If we press charges against him for attacking you then you will be dragged into it, and that isn't something I want to see. And if we charge him with defacing property, again you are the witness, and again you would be dragged in - and again, that isn't something I'm going to allow. Besides, he may be more use to us if we turn him loose. There's just a chance that whoever has been paying him may decide to use him again.'

'So that if we have him watched, we can see where he goes and what he does?' asked Rebecca.

Joshua nodded. 'Exactly.'

'It makes sense.'

A carriage rattled to a halt outside. Glancing out of the window Rebecca saw that it was hers.

'Until this evening, then,' she said, taking her leave of Joshua.

'Until this evening. Once I join you at the ball I will tell you everything I learn.'

'Oh! There you are! I was just beginning to worry,' said Louisa, as Rebecca returned to the house.

'I'm sorry I was so long,' said Rebecca.

'Never mind, my dear. You are here now.'

Rebecca smiled at the look of suppressed anticipation on Louisa's face. Too sweet to ask if Rebecca had managed to find her a fan in case she should seem demanding, Louisa was clearly wondering if Rebecca's shopping trip had been a success.

Rebecca opened her reticule and took out a small package, which she gave to Louisa.

Louisa took it and opened it to reveal the lace and ivory fan. Her face lit up. 'Oh! Rebecca! It's beautiful! So delicate! And so stylish!' She opened the fan with a flick of her wrist and delightedly wafted it to and fro.

'It will look lovely against your gown,' said Rebecca. 'The lace is so delicate the orange shade will shine through.'

'Yes, it will. Oh, thank you, my dear. It's perfect. Truly perfect.' Louisa fluttered her fan once more, until the chiming of the clock called her back to the present. 'But I must not keep you. You will be wanting to go up and dress. Susan has filled the hip bath for you, and laid out your gown. I, too, must get changed.'

Louisa hurried upstairs.

More slowly, Rebecca followed. She was glad to be able to retire to her room after her exciting afternoon.

The bedroom was welcoming. The heavy damask drapes had been drawn across the windows. A warming fire was burning in the grate, and the candles were shedding pools of light into every corner of the room.

Rebecca glanced towards the mantelpiece where an ormolu clock stood. She wanted to see if she had enough time to read a little more of her book in the bath, before she had to get dressed.

Yes, she had.

She took her book into the small dressing-room that led off from her bedroom, where Susan had filled her hip bath, and undressing she slipped into the rose-scented water. She breathed a sigh of relief. It had been an eventful few hours, and she was looking forward to some peace and quiet before she dressed to go out again.

She sank back into the water and luxuriated in the soothing warmth. Then, feeling pleasantly relaxed, she dried her hands on the towel she had draped over the edge of the bath and picked up The Italian, which she had left within reach. She indulged in a portion of the entertaining novel before washing herself and then stepping out of the hip bath, where she dried herself in front of the fire. Then she began to dress.

She had bought some lovely underclothes in the fashionable shops in Manchester and, with Susan's help, she proceeded to put them on: a cotton chemise and new-fangled drawers; silk stockings, fashionably embroidered at the ankles and held up by lace garters; and a light pair of stays.

Susan fastened her stays to a comfortable tightness, then it was time to put on her gown.

'How is Miss Louisa getting on?' asked Rebecca.

'She's finished dressing,' said Susan, who had gone to help Betsy with Louisa whilst Rebecca took her bath. 'She looks lovely,' said the young girl.

Rebecca was glad. She herself might be unlucky in love, but she hoped with all her heart that the same would not be true for her cousin.

She turned her attention to her new ball gown, which Susan was lifting off the bed. It was truly exquisite. Madame Dupont had excelled herself.

At that moment Betsy entered the room.

'Miss Louisa's compliments, and do you need any more help?' asked Betsy.

'No, thank you, Betsy,' said Rebecca.

Betsy eyed her dubiously. 'I don't know about these short sleeves,' she said, with the freedom of an old retainer. 'Pretty they may be, and fashionable as well, but a good pair of long sleeves would have been more sensible in the winter time, Miss Rebecca.'

'Perhaps,' remarked Rebecca. 'But long sleeves are too hot for dancing in.'

'You just make sure you take your shawl,' said Betsy. 'It won't do to go catching a cold. You'll miss all the coming parties and dinners, and you wouldn't want that.'

Rebecca's mouth quirked, but she dutifully promised to wear her shawl, and Betsy was mollified.

'There,' said Susan, standing back once the dress was fastened.

The gown was truly lovely. The gold silk glimmered in the candlelight and the short sleeves, trimmed with a row of the most delicate gold tassels, were exquisite. The high waist lent Rebecca height, and the demi-train added an air of elegance and style.

'I hope I can remember how the friseur said to do your hair,' said Susan somewhat nervously.

'I'm sure you will,' said Rebecca as Betsy departed.

She sat in front of her dressing-table and Susan proceeded to arrange her hair. Monsieur Toulouse had cut and shaped it, so that the maid had no difficulty in styling it.

Once it was done Rebecca examined the high chignon critically to make sure it was tidy. She fluffed the ringlets round her face, then thanking Susan she stood up.

'Your gloves, Miss Rebecca,' said Susan, handing Rebecca her long white evening gloves. 'And don't forget your shawl.'

Rebecca took up the beautiful spider-silk shawl and draped it elegantly over her shoulders. There would be time enough later, when she had reached Mrs Renwick's house and had warmed right through, to let it slip elegantly and fashionably down into the crook of her arms.

And then Rebecca was ready. Going downstairs she found Louisa already waiting for her. Louisa's eyes were sparkling, and in her new gown she looked lovely. Edward would be a fool if he did not want to marry her, Rebecca thought.

The clock chimed the hour. 'I believe we should be going,' said Rebecca.

'Yes,' agreed Louisa.

They went out to the carriage.

As they did so Rebecca felt a shiver of presentiment; as though something momentous was going to happen that very evening.

Then, dismissing the presentiment as nothing more than foolishness, she turned her attention to the evening to come.

Chapter Ten

As soon as Rebecca entered Mrs Renwick's house she looked round for Joshua. She was eager to see him and discover what he had learnt from Dunn. She could see no sign of him in the hall, however, and moved on to the impromptu ballroom, but here she fared no better. After scanning the brilliantly-dressed people for any sign of him, she realized he had not yet arrived.

'Oh, my, doesn't it look lovely,' said Louisa.

The ballroom did indeed look lovely. It was brightly decorated with such greenery as could be found so early in the year, all displayed in delightful porcelain vases. Together with the highly-polished mirrors, the glittering chandeliers, and the silk-and-satin clad guests, it was a splendid sight.

The most important people in Manchester were all gathered together, Rebecca noted with interest, turning her attention to the other guests. Mill owners, politicians, and a smattering of titled and other fashionable young men, together with their wives and sisters. There were also a number of eligible young ladies, fluttering around in their white muslin gowns.

Louisa's attention was soon claimed by Edward, and Rebecca was quickly accosted likewise.

'Miss Foster.'

Rebecca's relief vanished as she turned to see Mr Willingham. Ah, well, she would have to greet him politely.

'May I say you are looking truly exquisite this evening?' he went on, bowing over her hand.

She was made slightly uneasy by the way his eyes ran over her as he straightened up. There was something cold about him, and she had the feeling that he was looking at her in the way he would look at a beautiful painting or a fine piece of china - as though he was calculating her worth. However, she was a guest at the ball, and he was a respected gentleman, and so she ignored her distaste and thanked him politely for his compliment.

'And may I also say you are looking remarkably composed.'

Rebecca's eyebrows raised in surprise.

'It cannot be easy to be so calm after what happened this afternoon,' he said.

Her eyebrows raised still further.

'News travels fast,' he explained. 'Particularly among the mill owners. My mill is in Stockport, but I still get to hear of things that might be likely to affect business, and the unfortunate attack on you this afternoon is one of them.'

'I hardly think it is likely to affect your business,' she remarked.

'Forgive me, but if the Luddites are active again, it will affect everyone's business.'

'I don't believe — ' Rebecca started to say, before stopping herself.

'You don't believe?' prompted Mr Willingham, looking at her with a deceptively bland expression.

Rebecca remembered Joshua's warning, that Mr Willingham was a skilled conversationalist, and that he was used to getting information from people without them even realizing it. She did not know why, but she felt the less she told Mr Willingham about what she and Joshua suspected, the better. So instead of saying, "I don't believe it was the Luddites who attacked me", she said instead, 'I don't believe it was anything to worry about.'

'You will forgive me if I disagree. When so much beauty is attacked, it must worry the heart of each and every gentleman.' He made her a bow as he said it. 'But you must not take the Luddite threat lightly, Miss Foster. The Luddites are desperate people, and after the daubing on your mill wall, you must take care.'

'You know about that?'

'As I say, Miss Foster, there is little I don't know about what goes on in and around Manchester. It pays me to know. If you are sensible, you will not ignore them.'

'I assure you, you need have no concern on my account,' said Rebecca coolly. 'The whole matter was trivial, and not worth worrying about.'

'I'm glad to hear it. Even so, the Luddites are no respecters of persons and although this attack may have been trivial, the next one may be more serious.' He stopped himself, and then said, 'Not that there will be a next one, I'm sure. But it is perhaps worth remembering that the streets of Manchester are not always safe, particularly if one ventures off the major thoroughfares.'

How does he know I ventured off the major thoroughfares? wondered Rebecca. Was it really, as he said, that the local mill owners came to hear of anything unusual that happened to one of their number? Or could he be having her followed?

No, of course not. The idea was nonsensical. It was true he seemed to have an interest in her, but as she was an eligible young lady with a handsome dowry, to say nothing of owning half a mill, that in itself was perhaps not so surprising. But not even the most ardent suitor would have a young lady followed, and on so short an acquaintance.

A new and even more unwelcome thought occurred to her. Was it possible that he was in some way responsible for the attacks, both on Joshua and the mill?

But no. She dismissed the idea. Mr Willingham may have something to gain by paying court to her, if that court was successful, but he could have nothing to gain by setting fire to the mill, or by killing Joshua. On the contrary, he would have something to lose. Marsden mill provided his mill with the cotton it needed for weaving and dyeing, and if anything happened to disrupt Marsden mill, it would also disrupt the supply of the cotton. And Mr Willingham needed the cotton if his own business was to be run profitably.

And besides, he may not know she had wandered off the main streets at all. It may have been no more than a guess. So she replied to his comment with a polite nothing.

'No, indeed,' she said. 'It would not do to forget that the streets of Manchester are not always safe.'

He made her another bow. Then said, changing the subject, 'But all this talk of attacks and Luddites is out of place in a ballroom. You must forgive me for having mentioned it. It is only my concern for your well-being that prompted me to speak. But let us talk of other things. You have not forgotten that you have promised me your hand for the first dance, I hope?'

'I have not.'

He glanced at the small orchestra, who were just tuning their instruments. 'Before it begins, would you do me the very great favour of allowing me to introduce you to my mother?'

Rebecca readily assented. She found that she had little to say to Mr Willingham, and the diversion of meeting his mother was a welcome one. Besides, she and Louisa were engaged to take dinner with Mrs Willingham, and Rebecca was curious to see what sort of person she might be.

Mr Willingham led her over to the far side of the room, where an old woman with sharp, bright eyes was sitting. Mrs Willingham was swathed in black from head to foot, and wrapped up in a voluminous black shawl.

Mr Willingham made the introductions and Rebecca greeted his mother politely. But the same cold feeling came over her as it had done when Mr Willingham had paid her a compliment.

Willingham is ambitious, Joshua had told her, and she could well believe it. And she could also believe it of his mother. There was something cold and calculating about her. Even her continued wearing of mourning for a husband who had been dead for more than ten years seemed calculated, as though she wanted to stand out in any gathering and knew that wearing black would always allow her to do it. Of the late departed Mr Willingham she spoke only in the most scathing terms, leading Rebecca to realize she did not continue to wear mourning out of love or respect for her husband.

Rebecca made some observations on the size of the room and the elegance of the gathering, but Mrs Willingham did nothing to help her maintain a polite flow of conversation. Instead, she watched Rebecca with shrewd eyes, before finally saying, 'It has been a pleasure meeting you, Miss Foster.'

Rebecca flushed. The sentence, whilst seeming to be polite, was an unmistakable dismissal.

'Please don't mind my mother,' said Mr Willingham, seeing her flush, as he led her away. 'She is an old lady, and often in pain. It can make her rather abrupt.'

Rebecca made a polite rejoinder, but she did not altogether believe Mr Willingham, and felt he was making an excuse for his mother's bad manners.

However, the orchestra was striking up the opening chords of the first dance. She took his hand and together they went out onto the floor.

Rebecca was pleased to see that Louisa was there, curtseying to Edward - the two made a delightful couple, Rebecca thought - and then she caught sight of Joshua. He was looking magnificent in a black tailcoat and breeches, with a snow-white shirt and a simply tied cravat.

He was also dancing with Miss Serena Quentin.

Rebecca felt her stomach tie itself in knots. He seemed to have been paying a lot of attention to Miss Quentin recently.

But it was really none of her business, she told herself. She tried to fight down the feelings that filled her breast on seeing the two of them together.

But it was impossible.

The evening passed slowly. Rebecca had hoped that Joshua would ask her to dance, but her hand was rapidly claimed by other gentlemen and she could not in all politeness refuse them. But although the hours passed slowly, they did pass, and midnight drew ever nearer.

At last the clock showed a quarter to twelve.

It was still a little early to go and meet Joshua in the library, but fearing her hand might be sought for the next dance if she remained in the room, Rebecca slipped out into the corridor. Once there, she decided to make sure she knew where the library was, and having found the room she decided to stay.

The library was a handsome one. Although not as large as the library in a country house, it was nevertheless spacious and was well furnished with a large collection of books. Two chairs were placed one on either side of the fire, a sofa nestled against the far wall, and directly ahead of her was an attractive window seat, padded with a peacock-blue cushion. Matching peacock-blue curtains were tied back at either side of the window, allowing the light of the moon to shine faintly in at the window. It shone on two fine pieces of porcelain – a matched pair - which were set on the window ledge, one on each side of the embrasure, and complemented the light of the candles that glowed on the mantelpiece.

Rebecca amused herself by looking along the spines of the books then she selected a book of engravings, carrying it over to the window seat. It would give her something to look at until Joshua arrived.

She had hardly seated herself, however, when she heard footsteps coming towards the library. They did not belong to Joshua, they were quicker and lighter.

She did not want to have to make polite conversation with another guest and so she drew her legs up in front of her and pulled the curtains across the window and its seat. She hoped that whoever it was would not stay long.

The door opened and a gentleman came into the room.

Mr Willingham, she thought in surprise, as she saw him through a tiny gap in the drapes.

She was doubly glad she had managed to secrete herself behind the curtains. Mr Willingham's attentions were becoming marked, and she suspected he was looking for her. Seeing the library was empty he looked puzzled, but instead of going out again he moved further into the room.

Rebecca was annoyed. He was heading straight towards the window-seat and she suspected he meant to pull back the curtains.

But at that moment the door knob rattled and, distracted by the sound, he turned towards the door.

It opened, and Joshua walked in.

Through the tiny gap in the curtain, Rebecca could see that Mr Willingham and Joshua were looking at each other with expressions of barely concealed dislike.

'Kelling,' said Mr Willingham stiffly after a moment.

'Willingham,' said Joshua, making him a slight bow.

'What brings you to the library?' asked Mr Willingham. 'And in the middle of a ball?'

Joshua eyed him coldly. 'I could ask you the same question.'

'You could indeed,' said Mr Willingham smoothly. 'And I will be happy to tell you - if you come in and shut the door.'

Now why did Mr Willingham want Joshua to do that? wondered Rebecca.

She could tell by his face that Joshua was wondering the same thing.

Did Mr Willingham have some information about her assailant? Rebecca asked herself. Was that why he wanted Joshua to close the door? Did he have something sensitive to say? It would certainly fit in with the things he had said to her earlier in the evening.

Joshua seemed to suspect something of the same sort. He stepped further into the room and closed the door softly behind him.

'Well, Willingham? Do you have something to say to me?'

'I do indeed.' Mr Willingham indicated a chair.

Joshua glanced at the chair and then looked back at Mr Willingham. 'Thank you, but I'll stand.'

'As you wish,' said Mr Willingham. He took his cue from Joshua and remained standing himself. 'I understand you've been having trouble at your mill. A Luddite slogan painted on the wall. A fire.'

'And how would you know about those things?' Joshua asked curiously.

'Let's just say, a little bird told me.'

Joshua's glance hardened. 'If you've something to say to me, Willingham, say it. Otherwise, don't waste my time.'

'My, my, we are in a hurry,' said Mr Willingham.

Joshua turned to walk out of the door.

'I wouldn't do that if I were you, Kelling,' said Mr Willingham.

There was something in his tone that made Rebecca sit bolt upright. It was something chilling.

Through the crack in the curtains she saw Joshua turn round.

And then to her horror she saw Mr Willingham pull out a gun.

She stifled a gasp. From her vantage point she could only see Mr Willingham's back but the gilded mirror on the wall showed her his front clearly, and she could see without any shadow of a doubt that he was holding a pistol.

Thank goodness he hadn't realized she was concealed behind the curtains, after all.

Joshua's eyes went to the pistol and then back to Mr Willingham. 'So it was you,' he said.

'Not me personally,' said Mr Willingham smoothly.

'Of course not,' said Joshua scathingly. 'You wouldn't have the courage to do anything personally. Painting slogans, starting a fire - even attacking a woman. They are cowardly acts, admittedly, but even so, far too daring for you.'

'I'd remind you, Kelling, that I'm the one holding the gun,' said Mr Willingham angrily.

'And just what do you intend to do with it?' asked Joshua with contempt. 'As soon as you fire it, people will come running from all directions. True, you might manage to kill me, but you'll be caught red handed. Give it up.'

'Give it up? When I hold all the cards? You're right, people will come running when they hear a shot, but what of it? All I have to do is drop the gun, run out of the library, turn round and run towards it again, waiting only long enough to make sure someone witnesses me entering the library just ahead of them. They will simply think I have heard the shot and come running, like everyone else. It is just that I will be the first person to get here. And when I do, I will find you shot dead - killed by Luddite agitators.'

'Who will believe a story like that?' asked Joshua in disgust.

'Everyone. I'm a well-respected member of the community. If I see a rough-looking man with a curious loping gait leaving through the window, and if it comes to light - as it will - that your mill has recently been targeted by Luddites, then the authorities will know who to blame. They will mount a search, and unless I'm very much mistaken they will not find it difficult to discover the man, and to find that he is in possession of a tin of red paint.'

'You've thought it all out!'

'Of course I have. You don't think I'd leave anything to chance in a matter as important as this? The man will duly be arrested. I will testify that he is the person I saw leaving through the window - and the lovely Miss Foster will of course testify to the fact that he was the man who attacked her on the streets.'

Rebecca felt her anger rise as she realized the part she was expected to play in all this, the part of unwitting dupe.

Joshua's face darkened at the mention of her name. 'I suggest you leave Miss Foster out of this,' he said.

'You're not in a position to suggest anything,' said Mr Willingham, but he took a step backwards all the same. He raised the gun intimidatingly.

Rebecca's heart missed a beat. For all Joshua's high-handed ways, she could not bear to see him in danger. But even as she thought it she noted the fact that Mr Willingham's step backwards had brought him closer to the curtains. Her mind worked quickly and she realized that if Mr Willingham would only take one more step backwards he would be within her reach.

But what could she do against him, even if she could reach him? And without putting Joshua at risk?

'Why, Willingham?' demanded Joshua. 'It doesn't make sense. Why did you hire someone to paint a Luddite slogan on the mill wall? Why did you pay someone to start a fire, and to attack Miss Foster? What can you possibly hope to gain?'

That's right, Joshua, keep him talking, thought Rebecca, casting round for some way of helping him that would not get him killed. If she tried something and failed then the gun would go off and Joshua would be finished.

She thought of hitting him over the head with her book, but it was too slim to do him any harm.

'If you shoot me, it won't benefit you in any way,' Joshua was saying. 'It won't get you cheaper cotton to use in your weaving mill. So what is the point?'

'Cheaper cotton?' mocked Mr Willingham. 'Are you really so short-sighted? Do you still not see? I don't want cheaper cotton, I want your mill. With your cotton mill and my weaving and dyeing mill, I will have control of the whole production process. That means a drop in costs, and a huge rise in profits.'

'But killing me won't get you that,' said Joshua. 'My share of the mill doesn't go to you if I die.'

Mr Willingham smirked. 'I know. It goes to the lovely Rebecca.'

Rebecca had to bite back an angry exclamation.

'How in Hades do you know that?' asked Joshua, taking a step forward.

'I know which firm of London lawyers Jebediah Marsden used. It wasn't difficult to bribe one of the clerks to tell me the terms of his will,' said Mr Willingham, taking a step back.

Rebecca recalled the unctuous clerk who had let them into Mr Wesley's office. She had thought there was something shifty about him, and she was in no doubt that he was the clerk who had been bribed.

'And he, I suppose, was responsible for the attacks on me in London.'

Mr Willingham shook his head. 'He would not have been capable of it - sneaking is his forte, not daring action - but it was another low-life in my pay.'

'Another mystery explained,' said Joshua. 'Even so . . . even though my share goes to Rebecca, I don't see how . . . ' And then his face changed. 'You mean to marry her. Once you kill me, my share will go to her, and once you marry her it will pass to you, as part of her dowry. Giving you control of the mill. But you're mad if you think she'll do it. Rebecca will never marry you.'

Rebecca's heart soared as she heard the words. There was something in Joshua's expression that suggested he felt much more than the scorn he might have been expected to feel at Mr Willingham's belief she would marry him. There was a look of contempt that told her he respected her, as well as a flash of jealousy that made her wonder, against her better judgement, if his feelings for her had changed over the last few weeks, becoming deeper and more complex; in fact, if they matched her feelings for him.

Mr Willingham spoke dryly:

'Rebecca won't get a choice. You can't seriously believe I intend to let her decide for herself? I shall propose, of course, next week, after she has dinner with my mother and myself —'

'She won't accept you.'

'No. I don't suppose she will. Which is why I intend to have a special licence in my pocket and a clergyman standing by. She will marry me before she leaves the house, or she will not leave it at all.'

Rebecca, seeing at last how she could help, seized one of the jugs that decorated the embrasure and leapt to her feet. Standing on the window seat she pulled back the curtain. The noise distracted Mr Willingham, who looked round, and Joshua, seeing his chance, lost only a fraction of a second in surprise before hurling himself at Mr Willingham. Mr Willingham, turning his attention back to Joshua, lifted the gun - and Rebecca brought the jug crashing down on his head.

He stood for one moment, and Rebecca thought her efforts had been wasted - but then he swayed and fell, crumpling up in a heap on the floor.

Joshua caught the gun as it dropped out of his hand and checked that Mr Willingham, now lying prone, was really out cold, and then turned to Rebecca, who was still standing on the window-seat.

The strain of the last ten minutes, coupled with her cramped conditions - which had left her with pins and needles in her legs, so that they could barely hold her - made her begin to sway. Joshua held out his arms, and as she lost her balance he caught her in his strong embrace.

'Becky,' he said, with such a look in his eyes that she felt herself melting.

'Josh,' she said breathlessly, feeling the heat of his body against her own.

He looked into her eyes for a long moment. Then, as if remembering she had been through something of an ordeal, he carried her over to one of the chairs and set her down gently in it before kneeling in front of her.

'Your hands are cold,' he said. He began to chafe them.

'It was cold in the window embrasure,' she said. 'And I forgot my shawl. It's still in the ballroom.'

He moved her chair closer to the fire.

'But what were you doing behind the curtains in the first place?' he asked as he continued to chafe her hands.

Briefly, she explained why she had taken refuge there.

'It's a good thing you did. Otherwise I may well be —'

'Don't, Josh,' she said with a shudder, putting a finger to his lips. 'Don't even say it.'

He took her hand and kissed her fingers, then, turning it over, he kissed the palm and the inside of her wrist.

Could his feelings have changed? she wondered again as the most intoxicating shiver washed over her. Could they have developed into something as deep and sincere as her own? For she was no longer in any doubt as to the nature of her own feelings for Joshua. She was in love with him.

Oh, yes, she was in love with him, and no matter how hard she had tried to deny it, she knew that she had been so for a long time.

To begin with, she had felt no more for him than physical attraction, but her feelings had soon begun to undergo a transformation. When she had been caught in the path of the charging horse in London and he had pushed her to safety she had been filled with a sense of security that had warmed her through. His tenderness towards her following the incident had surprised her, revealing that there was a gentler side to his nature than the one he generally showed the world. His concern for her reputation had earned her esteem, and his obvious devotion to her beloved grandfather had earned her affection and her gratitude. His drive and ambition had struck a chord in her own nature - she was not Jebediah's granddaughter for nothing! - and his ruthlessness, once she had realized it did not spill over into cruelty, had roused her respect; for she knew it would be impossible to succeed in his chosen sphere of business without it.

And yet all these feelings, whilst explaining some of what she felt for him, did not explain it all, for she felt something she had never felt for any man before: that she wanted to join herself to him - in every way.

She felt a warm tingling sensation spread through her as the realization hit her with full force.

How strange. She had never thought, when she had first met him at *The Queen's Head*, that she would fall in love with him, but despite the fact he was stubborn and determined – or perhaps because of it - she had done so.

And yet, did Joshua love her? Or was he still resolute in his determination never to offer her his hand again?

'Rebecca,' he said, stroking his fingers over her palms in the most delicious way, 'I asked you once before,' he said, his eyes glowing in the mixed fire-and-candlelight —

A low groan interrupted him.

He cursed under his breath.

Dropping her hand he turned in the direction of the noise.

Rebecca, too, turned her head, and saw that Mr Willingham was starting to stir. He had been knocked out when she had crashed the jug down on his head but that was all. And now he was coming round.

Rising from his knees, Joshua crossed the room to Mr Willingham. Untying his cravat he quickly bound Willingham's hands and feet, roping them together with the voluminous material so that Mr Willingham was held fast.

'Odgers is in the ballroom,' he said to Rebecca.

'Odgers?' she asked in surprise.

Joshua gave a wide smile. 'He is dressed in some of my old clothes, and though he's undoubtedly an ugly customer he is just about able to pass for a guest!'

Rebecca felt her own mouth twitch. The sight of Odgers as a guest at the ball must be a sight indeed.

'Bring him here, whilst I keep an eye on Willingham,' said Joshua. 'He can help me take him out to the carriage.'

'It will cause a stir,' said Rebecca with a frown. 'Can you not think of another way of getting him out of the house, without embarrassing Mrs Renwick in her own home?'

'There won't be any embarrassment,' Joshua reassured her. 'Once Odgers joins me I'll unbind Willingham and together we can help him out to the carriage - he's still groggy and is not likely to offer any resistance. If anyone sees us they will simply assume we are helping our friend, who has taken too much to drink.'

Rebecca nodded. He was right. Young men being carried out to their carriages befuddled with wine was such a normal sight that no one would worry about it. 'I'll fetch Odgers at once.'

She slipped out of the room and into the ballroom. There was no sign of Odgers. But a glance into the supper room showed him helping himself to a large plate of oyster patties and a couple of veal and ham pies.

Going unobtrusively over to his side, Rebecca said, 'You are wanted in the library.'

Without turning a hair Odgers put down his plate and made a discreet exit.

Rebecca was just about to follow him when she was joined by Louisa.

'There you are, my dear. I thought I had lost you! It is such a crush I thought I would never find you again. And I did so want to see you. I have some wonderful news!'

Rebecca's sprits sank. Fond as she was of her cousin she did not want to be distracted, particularly not now. But she had no choice. She could not ignore Louisa, and so instead she made an effort to concentrate on what her cousin was saying.

'Would you believe it?' said Louisa, hands clasped and eyes shining. 'Edward has just asked me to marry him.'

'Oh, Louisa, that's wonderful!' said Rebecca. She was genuinely happy for her cousin, and her enthusiasm was real.

'I can hardly believe it,' said Louisa. 'It has all been so sudden. But it is wonderful nonetheless.'

'Have you told Emily yet?'

'No. I am leaving it to Edward to break the news - although he says she already suspects. Oh! It has all been so exciting! But do you know, my dear, I feel ever so tired, and I believe I have a headache coming on. Would you mind if I called for the carriage? I think I am in need of a long lie down.'

Rebecca's spirits sank. She wanted to find out whether Willingham had been put safely in a carriage, and even more than that she wanted to know what Joshua had been about to say to her when Willingham had groaned.

I asked you once . . . he had begun, but what had he been about to say?

She hardly dared hope he had been about to renew his proposal. Surely a man as ruthless as Joshua would not, after declaring he would never offer her his hand again, change his mind? But even so, she could not help hoping . . .

There was nothing for it, however. If Louisa was feeling ill, they must leave.

Besides, she comforted herself, Joshua would be attending their card party on the following evening. It would not be long before she saw him again.

But despite her reasonable comforting, she found that the following evening seemed a lifetime away.

Nevertheless, it could not be helped.

'Of course I don't mind,' she said, with more tact than truthfulness. 'We will call for the carriage to be brought round right away.'

Together she and Louisa went out into the hall.

She had thought they might see Joshua half-carrying, half-supporting Mr Willingham out to the carriage, but there was no sign of him in the hall. Either he and Odgers had already gone, or they had not yet had a chance to leave the library. Well, whichever it was, they would soon be on their way, putting Willingham where he could do no more harm.

The Marsden carriage was brought round, and before long she and Louisa were in the carriage as it rattled through the streets, back to their rented Manchester home.

I asked you once . . . she thought, looking out of the window at the darkened streets as she recalled Joshua's words.

Yes. He had asked her once.

The question was, would he ask her again?

Serena Quentin's handsome face was marred by a scowl. Despite her best endeavours she had been unable to force Mr Kelling into a compromising position. He had managed to avoid every trap she had laid for him during the course of the evening, and what was worse, he had done it with a mocking smile on his lips - as though he saw through all her subterfuges and meant to thwart her, she thought angrily.

What right did he have to resist her charms? And, more importantly, what right did he have to turn her into a laughing stock? For if she did not manage to bring him to heel she would be just that: a laughing stock. Lavinia Madely would see to that.

Catching sight of Lavinia at that moment, her anger was fuelled by the scorn in Lavinia's eye. Throwing back her shoulders she decided bold action was necessary and, walking defiantly out of the room, she went in search of Joshua.

She did not have far to go. No sooner had she reached the hall than she heard a door opening and, to her surprise, she saw Joshua emerging from the library. But it was not that which surprised her, it was the fact that, instead of walking out of the room in a natural fashion, he was half-supporting, half-carrying someone else.

Mr Willingham! she thought with a sudden shock.

Mr Willingham, who scarcely ever drank, and certainly never drank enough to render him incapable.

Her curiosity rose.

What was the meaning of it? And who was the second gentleman - if such a rough looking creature could be given that description - supporting Mr Willingham at the other side?

She shrank back as Joshua half-supported, half-carried Mr Willingham through the hall and out of the house.

And then fate played into her hands, for Mr Willingham suddenly rallied and made an effort to break away from his captors. As he did so he slipped on the highly-polished floor. He clutched at Joshua, trying to regain his footing, but it was no use. He was seized again and carried bodily out of the front door. At the same moment there was a slight clinking sound, and a flash of gold caught Serena's eye. Something had fallen from Joshua's hand.

His gold signet ring! Mr Willingham must have dislodged the precious item during his struggle. A plan already forming in her mind, she picked it up and examined it. It was the ring his godfather had given him. She remembered him telling her all about it when, on seeing the initial engraved on it, she had teasingly enquired who the lady might be. He had told her there was no lady in the case, and when she had playfully tried to take it from his finger he had resisted, saying the only lady he would ever permit to try on that ring was his future wife.

His future wife. He had said those very words. And what's more, Lavinia Madely had heard him.

A triumphant smile crossed her face. What did it matter if she had not been able to force Joshua into a compromising situation? She had been able to do something far better: avail herself of his signet ring.

She slipped it onto her long white finger. It was rather large, but never mind. It could be made to serve her purpose, and that was all she cared about.

Exultantly she swept back into the ballroom - only to discover, after much fruitless searching, that Miss Lavinia Madely had already left.

But no matter. Lavinia was due to attend Rebecca Foster's card party the following evening.

Serena, in triumphant mood, was prepared to wait.

Chapter Eleven

The following afternoon, Rebecca was sitting in the drawing-room, making plans for the mill. But it was no use. They could not hold her attention, and she put them aside before pacing restlessly across the room. Arriving at the fireplace she straightened the porcelain figurines on the mantelpiece before crossing the room again to straighten the cushions on the sofa. She moved restlessly from the sofa to the piano, where she straightened the music on the stand. And all the time her thoughts were filled with the events of the night before.

She remembered it all so clearly. Mr Willingham's treachery, her own prompt actions, Joshua's mastery of the situation, and then the aftermath: Joshua's tender looks, the way he had taken her hands, his impassioned words. Could it be possible? Could his feelings towards her have changed? Could he love her as much as she loved him? She hardly dared to hope it. And yet why else would he have stroked her hands so tenderly? Why else spoken those impassioned words?

Oh, why had Louisa had to have a headache the night before? she asked herself. Chiding herself a moment later for the unkind thought. If it was as she suspected, then Joshua would speak to her that evening at the card party. And if not . . . No, she would not even think such a thing.

She went over to the mantelpiece and straightened the ormolu clock.

Fortunately - for there was nothing left to straighten! - Louisa bustled into the room at that moment, saying, 'Oh, my dear, can you lend me your assistance? The servants are carrying the card tables into the sitting-room, but I cannot decide on the best arrangement.'

Rebecca was only too glad to offer her help, and before long the tables had been successfully organized. Then there was the greenery to be arranged - the two ladies would have liked to provide flowers, but the season unfortunately provided very little in this way - and the catering arrangements to be checked. There were the footmen to instruct, the wine to be seen to and the packs of cards to be placed on each table, so that all in all Rebecca was kept very busy.

By five o'clock everything was ready, and Rebecca and Louisa sat down to a light tea - a cup of the refreshing beverage, taken with a little seed cake - before retiring to their rooms to dress.

Joshua's fingers fumbled as he made a second attempt at tying his cravat.

I should be looking forward to this evening, he told himself. I'm about to offer Becky my hand and to make her my betrothed.

If she will have me.

That was the thought that plagued him as he made a mess of yet another cravat. He gave it up in disgust and, wrenching it from his neck, threw it to the floor, where it landed on top of his first discarded effort.

He took up another freshly starched piece of linen and tried again.

It did not matter how many times he told himself that of course she would have him. That she loved him, as he loved her.

And when had he realized that? he asked himself. He did not know. It had crept up on him gradually, but it had begun the first time he had set eyes on her in the inn.

He gave a wry smile as he remembered how she had stood up to him. Oh, yes, she had impressed him even then. She had made him take notice of her, and not just as an intriguing face and a voluptuous set of curves, but as a person. Their following encounters had done nothing to diminish this fact, but had rather accentuated it. Over and over again she had refused to fall in with his wishes, and yet every time she had been right. How he had admired her for her courage in standing up to him. And he had admired her in a different way for taking an interest in the world around her, and for becoming involved in the mill. It may not have been convenient for him - nothing about Rebecca was ever convenient! - but she had taught him that men and women could be partners, something he had never realized before.

In her he had found his equal.

But when had these feelings turned to love? He did not know. That had been more subtle. But love it had become. He wanted her, needed her, in every way. He wanted to see her there beside him when he woke up in the morning; to take breakfast with her; to be tormented by her, delighted by her, and enraptured by her for the rest of his life. And all this would be his . . . if only she said yes.

Memories of her previous refusals returned to haunt him, but he resolutely put all such thoughts out of his mind and concentrated on his cravat.

Curse Brummell for making the wretched things fashionable! he thought unreasonably as his fingers, made clumsy with anticipation of the evening to come, refused to tie the required knot and a third cravat followed the first two onto the floor.

He almost gave into a temptation to ring the bell for his valet, but he fought it. He did not like being dressed by someone else, and although he kept a valet, the man was there to keep his clothes clean and boots polished, and nothing more. He took a deep breath, then began again. Abandoning all attempts to tie anything complicated, he settled for a simple barrel knot. Finally his fingers did what he wanted them to do, and the cravat was successfully tied.

Having succeeded with the most difficult part of his dress, he put on his waistcoat and shrugged on his tailcoat before inspecting himself in the cheval glass. He frowned. The one thing missing was his signet ring.

He could not think how he had come to lose it. No matter. He had set Odgers to looking for it. He had more important things to think of tonight.

Running his hands through his wild mane of hair, he picked up his greatcoat and went out to the waiting carriage.

'Oh, my dear, you do look very nice,' said Louisa appreciatively as the two ladies waited for their guests to arrive. Rebecca was dressed in an exquisitely simple high-waisted gown. Its skirt was of white satin and its bodice was of dark red. Dark red sleeves, decorated with a white ribbon, set it off to perfection. As a finishing touch, a dark red ribbon was threaded through Rebecca's ebony hair.

'Thanks to Susan's ministrations and Madame Dubois's hard work,' replied Rebecca with a smile. 'And you are looking radiant.'

'Do you think so?' asked Louisa, eyes shining. Her dress, an amber satin, had a double row of flounces round the hem, matched by a frill round the discreet neckline. 'You don't think it too fussy?'

'Not at all,' said Rebecca.

Louisa gave a sigh of relief. 'I do so like the frills - they are so pretty - but I was worried they might not be quite the thing. But you have set my mind at rest.'

'I'm sure Edward will find them delightful.'

'Oh, my dear, I am so happy!' said Louisa. 'I only hope I may soon see you as happy as I am.'

Rebecca flushed. Far from being happy, she was in an agony of suspense. Was it possible that her own love would have such a happy outcome? she wondered. Or had she read too much into Joshua's look, and made too much of his enigmatic words?

She did not know. And until she did, she could not be easy.

Her attention was fortunately soon taken up with receiving the guests for the card party, who slowly began to arrive. There was no Mr Willingham, despite the fact that he had been invited - by now, Rebecca hoped, he would be safely handed over to the local magistrate.

There was also no Joshua. As the time ticked by, Rebecca was seized by a feeling of uncertainty.

Surely he meant to come?

But of course he meant to come, she reassured herself. He must simply have been delayed - by business, perhaps, or by affairs connected with Mr Willingham's arrest. She must give her attention to her other guests until he arrived.

Having seen everyone settled round their card tables, amply supplied with refreshments, she slipped out of the room, meaning to give an order for more wine to be brought up. The party had proved successful and she did not want the supply to run low. But she was stopped short by the sight of Miss Serena Quentin talking to Miss Lavinia Madely, for Miss Quentin was proudly displaying a ring.

Surely she had seen that ring before? thought Rebecca with a lurch beneath her breast. The gold flashed in the glow of the candles, and the letter "J" caught the light. Rebecca closed her eyes, before opening them again and steeling her nerve. For it was Joshua's ring that Miss Quentin was wearing.

At that moment, Miss Quentin turned round, and with an arch smile, said, 'Miss Foster! What a surprise you gave me! I did not see you there. But it is a good thing you are here, for you may be one of the first to congratulate me! I am not meant to say anything at present, but I cannot resist. Mr Kelling and I are to be married!'

Rebecca felt as though she had been stabbed.

'Married?' she asked. Her voice came out as a whisper.

'Yes,' crowed Serena. 'Is it not splendid news? I am so happy I could cry!'

'It doesn't look much like a betrothal ring,' put in Miss Lavinia Madely spitefully. Her mouth was pursed and she looked severely displeased.

'Of course not,' said Miss Quentin, her air of triumph unshaken. 'That will come later. Diamonds, I think, or possibly emeralds, to match my "heavenly green eyes" - for that is what Mr Kelling calls them,' she said. 'But he wanted to give me something to be going on with, and what better than his beloved signet ring? I do declare, it seems like only yesterday he was forbidding me to take it from his finger, and saying that only his future wife would be permitted to do such a thing. And now I am his future wife, and I am wearing his ring!' She looked at Rebecca archly. 'Well, Miss Foster? Are you not going to congratulate me?'

'Of . . . of course,' said Rebecca. She had to acknowledge the meaning of the ring, but her mind cried out against it. Joshua? Betrothed to Miss Quentin? It couldn't be.

And yet, why not? Miss Quentin was extremely handsome. Joshua had often been in her company. They were both ruthless. Why should he not have offered her his hand?

Because she had thought . . .

But she had been mistaken, she told herself harshly.

She had hoped he was in love with her - hoped he had been about to offer her his hand - but the hope had proved false.

There was a rushing sound in her ears, and she felt tears stinging the back of her eyes. 'If you will excuse me,' she said, 'I need to instruct the butler.'

And drawing herself up to her full height she continued on her way with her head held high.

Once out of sight of the two young ladies, however, her shoulders slumped as she took in the full enormity of the situation. Joshua was betrothed to Miss Quentin. She would not have believed it possible. And yet Miss Quentin had been wearing his ring.

Her head was throbbing; her heart aching; and she wanted nothing more than to retire to her room, to lay down on her bed, and to shut out the nightmare. But it could not be. She could not retire. She and Louisa had a house full of guests, and she must see to their needs, entertain them with light-hearted conversation, and appear to be cheerful and perfectly at ease.

Her heart shrivelled at the thought of it, but it could not be helped. Louisa had been looking forward to the card party since it had first been decided upon, and Rebecca did not want to spoil the evening for her, particularly as Louisa was so radiant. No. She must put on a bright smile and behave as though nothing was wrong.

The one comfort was that Joshua had not attended the party, and Rebecca fervently hoped that he would not now arrive. To congratulate him on his betrothal would be more than she could bear. If fortune favoured her his business would keep him away from the party, and it would not be long then before she returned to Cheshire. Once there she would have no call to see him - she could simply declare that she had seen all she needed to at the mill and that she had decided to conduct her future business with Joshua by post. And then she would be able to recover in the safety and seclusion of her country house.

Or at least, she would be able to try. For she could not conceal from herself that it would be impossible to recover from such a blow. On the outside, perhaps. But on the inside? Never.

She shook her head in an effort to drive away such hopeless thoughts. Allowing herself a few minutes in an ante-room to collect herself, she went on to instruct the butler before returning to the sitting-room, where the card tables were in full swing.

'Ah! There you are,' beamed Louisa. Then her smile faded and she said in concern, 'My dear. What is it? Are you ill? You don't look quite the thing.'

'It's nothing,' said Rebecca. She tried to speak reassuringly, but her voice came out shakily.

'It is the excitement,' said Louisa in concern. 'All these parties are delightful, but they are tiring nonetheless.'

Rebecca did not correct Louisa. That worthy lady would discover the reason for her unhappiness soon enough, but until that time she did not want to cause Louisa distress. Nor, she was forced to admit, did she want to cause herself distress. For if Louisa knew that Joshua was betrothed to Miss Quentin, she would undoubtedly offer sympathy, and that was something Rebecca could not bear.

'The one disappointment is that Joshua is not here,' went on Louisa. 'Still, I expect - oh, but I was wrong. Here is Joshua now.'

Rebecca felt her heart give a lurch and felt a flush spreading over her cheeks. She turned away in confusion, knowing she was not equal to seeing him, to greeting him. So, making an excuse she crossed the card room with as much unconcern as she could muster and went out of the door at the far end.

Her escape, however, was short lived, for no sooner had she closed the door behind her than it opened again, and Joshua came through.

Why did he have to look so devastatingly attractive? thought Rebecca in an agony of feeling. And why did he have to look at her in that intimate way, with his eyes dancing and his mouth curving into a tantalizing smile? Why could he not have looked at her remotely? Why could he not have been austere? But that had never been Joshua's way. And it was not his way now, not even when he was betrothed to Miss Quentin.

'Running away from me, Rebecca?' he asked teasingly, catching hold of her hands and turning her to face him.

'No. Of course not,' she said brightly; nevertheless reclaiming her hands and putting them resolutely down at her side. To have Joshua touching her was too painful, now that she knew he was betrothed to someone else.

She had hoped to avoid speaking to him about his betrothal, knowing how painful she would find it. But the terrible tension that had gripped her since Joshua had walked into the card room must have some release, and she realized it could only be accomplished by congratulating him.

How she could bring herself to do it she did not know, but she knew that if she did not speak the tension would become unbearable. She must do what had to be done; get it over with; so that she could put it behind her, instead of having it looming endlessly in front of her.

'I am glad you are here,' she began. She stopped, clenching her hands into fists at her sides, curling them so tightly that her nails bit into her palms. 'I want to be the first to congratulate you.'

He looked surprised. 'Congratulate me?' he asked.

'Yes.' She smiled, hoping the smile did not look as brittle as it felt. It had cost her an enormous effort, and she prayed that the effort had not been in vain. 'On your betrothal.'

'My betrothal?' He sounded even more surprised.

'To Miss Quentin,' said Rebecca.

There. The words were out. She had said them.

But far from releasing the tension that had built up inside her, they seemed to make it worse.

To her surprise, Joshua did not thank her for her kind words. Instead his face darkened, and she realized he was angry.

But of course. Miss Quentin had said she was not meant to speak of the betrothal. Joshua, presumably, had wanted to tell her of it himself.

'Don't be angry with her,' she said. 'I know she was not meant to speak of it yet, but she was so overjoyed she could not help herself.'

Rebecca felt her courage sinking rapidly, and her legs felt as though they wanted to fold under her. But she refused to give way. Summoning her pride and dignity to her aid, she said, 'I am delighted for you.'

As she spoke the words she felt as though a part of her was dying.

But she must concentrate. Joshua was speaking. And yet they were not the words she had expected to hear.

'I am betrothed to Miss Quentin, and you are delighted?' he asked, his eyes searching her face.

His voice was surprisingly hollow, and on his face she saw what seemed to be a look of devastation. But of course it could not be that. She must be misreading him. After all, it would not be the first time she had done so. She had thought he was in love with her, and she had been wrong then. She must be wrong about this as well.

She made a supreme effort. 'Yes,' she said with her brightest smile. 'I am.'

What looked like a wave of utter desolation swept over his face, and for one moment she wondered if there had been a ghastly mistake.

But no. How could there have been? If there had been a mistake he would have told her so. He would have said, You are wrong. I am not betrothed to Miss Quentin. It's you I love, Becky. But he said nothing of the kind.

His voice, when at last he spoke, was unemotional to the point of deadness. 'In that case, there is no more to be said.'

And turning on his heel he went back into the card room, closing the door behind him.

All the tension that had held Rebecca rigidly upright throughout the encounter suddenly flooded out of her, and her legs folded beneath her. She could do nothing about it and, worn out by her struggles, she collapsed into a Hepplewhite chair.

She was completely drained. Congratulating Joshua had taken her last ounce of strength and her last grain of courage. Still, she consoled herself, it was over. The worst was behind her. She had managed to congratulate Joshua on his betrothal. She would not need to do so again.

She sat there for some minutes before realizing she must stir herself. She should go back into the card room and attend to her guests.

With difficulty she roused herself. Standing up, she smoothed her skirt, lifted her chin, and pinched her cheeks to put a little colour into them. Then she returned to her guests. As she passed between the tables at the card party, smiling and talking, no one would have guessed from her manner that she was concealing a great hurt. But it was there inside her, making every word an effort and every smile a source of the most unbearable pain.

Joshua strode back through the card room neither seeing nor hearing anything that was going on around him. All he could see, in his mind's eye, was Rebecca's smile when she had congratulated him on his betrothal to Miss Quentin.

Miss Quentin, of all people! That hard, spoilt, calculating monster! He would not have married Miss Quentin if she had been the last woman on earth. How could Rebecca have believed it? Did she not know that he was in love with her? Obviously not. And equally obviously she did not care.

He had got it all wrong, he thought, as he ran his hand through his mane of dark blond hair, almost consumed by despair. He had thought her feelings for him had changed. He had thought she had come to love him as much as he had come to love her. There had been something in her expression the night before, when together they had overcome Mr Willingham, that had made his heart soar. But it had been nothing, he saw that now. Nothing but his own wishful thinking, ascribing to her feelings she did not possess.

'Joshua!'

Louisa's voice roused him from his reverie.

'Why, what is it?' she asked in horror as he turned to look at her. 'You look terrible. Is something wrong at the mill?'

Catching sight of himself in a looking-glass he realized at once why Louisa was concerned. His eyes were wild, and there was a look of utter desolation on his face.

He made an effort to restore his features to normal. With limited success. 'It is nothing,' he said. 'Just a small problem that has cropped up.' Which, whilst not truthful, at least reassured Louisa and removed the worried look from her face.

'You work too hard,' she said. 'But at least you can enjoy yourself this evening. Rebecca will be back before long - she has just gone to see to the refreshments.'

Joshua made a polite rejoinder and to his relief Louisa moved on to her other guests. He did not feel equal to her well-meant conversation about Rebecca tonight.

But there was one thing he did feel equal to. It was obvious Miss Quentin had been spreading rumours about a supposed betrothal, and he meant to put a stop to them before they did any more harm.

It did not take him long to find her. She was preening herself before one of the gilded mirrors in the dining-room, where the supper had been laid out. Fortunately, as it was too early for supper, no one else was in the room.

'Mr Kelling,' she said, startled, turning round as he opened the door. Her right hand closed guiltily over her left hand, as she tried to surreptitiously slip the signet ring from her finger.

But the movement, surreptitious though it was, drew his attention, and he caught sight of a tell-tale gleam of gold.

'My ring,' he said grimly.

The reason for its disappearance was now obvious. He had not lost it, as he had suspected. Miss Quentin had taken it.

'I . . . was going to give it back to you,' she said, trying to speak boldly but betraying her anxiety by a wobble in her voice. 'I found it,' she went on hurriedly, 'on the floor, after you'd taken Mr Willingham out to his carriage last night.'

'And you did not think to return it to me?' asked Joshua with disdain.

'I . . . I was going to, but —'

'But you thought you would use it to convince people that we were betrothed instead,' he said with contempt.

'I never —'

'Good,' said Joshua, cutting across her protestation of innocence. 'Because if such a rumour were to get out, it would inevitably leave you looking ridiculous when no marriage was forthcoming. And no,' he said, seeing the direction her thoughts were taking, 'I wouldn't spring to your assistance by making you a genuine offer in order to protect your reputation. If you were thinking anything of the sort then you're a fool.'

Miss Quentin, who looked as though she had been about to speak, was silenced. One look at Joshua's implacable face told her that he would never allow himself to be manipulated, as she had supposed.

'And now I suggest you give the ring to me and then return to the other guests,' said Joshua. 'I have a mind for peace and quiet, and I have a mind to find it here.'

Miss Quentin's eyes hardened, and she looked as though she might protest, but a look from Joshua changed her mind and she handed over the ring. Then, accepting her dismissal, she retained just enough spirit to exit with her head held high.

So that is why Becky though I was engaged, though Joshua, turning the ring in his hands before putting it back on his little finger.

If she had been dismayed at the idea he would have gone to her there and then, and told her that it was not true. But far from being dismayed she had been delighted. She had congratulated him with a warm smile on her face.

He threw himself down into a chair. It was over, he thought bitterly. All chance of the betrothal he had longed for had been smashed by Rebecca's warm smile and even warmer words. His hopes and dreams had been shattered in an instant. He let out a low groan. If he had heard of her betrothal it would have ripped the heart out of his body.

But on hearing of his betrothal, she had been delighted.

Rebecca appeared to be happy and at ease as she bid her guests goodnight. But she was heartsore. She longed for the release of retiring to her room, where she could give way to the emotions that were churning inside her. All through the evening she had hidden them, but the strain had been enormous and she felt that if the last guests did not soon leave her smile would crack and her true feelings would be revealed.

She had just bid Mr and Mrs Braithwaite goodnight, when a sudden change in the air made her look up and her heart missed a beat. There was Joshua, taking his leave of Louisa. In a moment he would come to her and she must be ready to utter a few polite words, thanking him for attending the party and hoping he had had a pleasant time.

She took a deep breath in order to steady her rapidly beating pulse and prepared herself to do so. It would be the last ordeal of the evening, she consoled herself. Once it was over, she had only to say goodnight to the few remaining guests and then she could retire to her room, where her turbulent emotions could be given free rein.

'Rebecca,' he said formally, bowing over her hand.

'Joshu —'

She broke off. A gleam of gold on his finger had caught her eye as he raised her hand to his lips.

'Your ring!' she exclaimed. She turned astonished eyes up to his.

'I have reclaimed it,' he said with a twist of the mouth. 'I am sorry to disappoint you, Rebecca, but Miss Quentin and I are not betrothed.'

'Not . . . not betrothed?'

She could not help it. A tide of relief washed over her face, revealing her true feelings.

'You're not disappointed?' he asked, a look of hope appearing on his face.

'No,' she whispered.

'We cannot talk here.' He drew her aside, taking her through into the drawing-room and closing the door behind them. Then, pulling her to him, he took her hands between his own and stroked her fingers in the most heart-wrenching way. 'Why not?' he asked, looking down at her as though he longed to devour every inch of her.

'Because . . . ' She gulped.

'Yes, Becky?'

'Because . . . ' She took a deep breath. It was the moment of truth. She turned her face up to his. 'Because I'm in love with you.'

'Oh, Becky,' he groaned, then pulling her to him he pressed his lips to her own.

'Rebecca,' he said, looking deeply into her eyes when at last he let her go, 'I have asked you twice before to marry me and you refused me, but everything has changed since then. This time I am not only offering you my hand, I am offering you my heart as well. I am in love with you.'

'I know.' She went willingly into his arms. 'And this time . . . '

'Yes, Rebecca?' he asked, looking down at her with a mixture of love and longing in his tawny eyes.

'This time,' she said, 'I accept.'

'There's still one thing I don't understand,' said Rebecca, when Joshua finally loosed her from his embrace. 'How did Serena come by your ring?'

'As to that, it is easily answered. Mr Willingham dislodged it when he struggled to get away - he came round just as Odgers and I were half-carrying, half-dragging him through the hall. I didn't notice at the time, but Serena did. She picked it up —'

' — and used it to make mischief,' finished Rebecca. It fit in with what she knew of Serena only too well. She recalled how Serena had been showing off the ring to Lavinia Madeley when she had stumbled upon them, and guessed that some sort of wager had been involved. It would not have been the first time Serena and Lavinia had placed bets in such a manner, challenging each other to win various bachelors' attentions.

'But of course, her plan could never have worked,' said Joshua. 'In fact, I don't believe she'd have even attempted it if she'd realized I was in love with you.'

'When did you know?' Rebecca asked.

'That I loved you?'

She nodded.

He pulled her onto the sofa beside him, and wrapped his arm lovingly around her waist.

'It's difficult to say for sure.'

'When Mr Willingham attacked you?'

'No. Long before that. I think I must have loved you when I asked you to marry me the first time, back in London, when we were at the Frost Fair.'

She turned to look at him in surprise. 'But I thought you were offering me your hand because you had compromised me.'

'So did I. But I think I must have already been half in love with you, even though I didn't know it. I don't believe I would have offered you my hand otherwise.'

'Not even to save my reputation?'

'Once it was in jeopardy, yes - I was very attached to Jebediah, and I wouldn't have wanted to bring disgrace down on his granddaughter's head - but not before. Lacy might have seen us together at *The Queen's Head* but I knew he was a coward, and that he wouldn't talk. And as to the idea of someone else seeing us together, that was pure speculation. If someone had seen us together, and had been about to noise it abroad, then yes, I would have offered you my hand, but not until then. Not unless I'd known somewhere deep inside me that I wanted to make you my wife.'

Rebecca sighed. 'I was very tempted to accept —'

'You were?' It was his turn to be surprised.

She nodded. 'Yes. I couldn't think why. But now I know. It was because, underneath, I was already falling in love with you.'

'And yet I'm glad you didn't accept my hand then. I hadn't come to see you as my equal, I must admit, I did not want you to involve yourself in the mill. It was only later, when we worked together, that I came to do so. The way you stood up to me left me in no doubt that you were a force to be reckoned with and, more than that, I was forced to acknowledge that your ideas made sense. Even so, I resisted seeing you as an equal. But once you'd rescued me from the fire I could deny it no longer, because without your help I would have died.'

It was a sobering thought.

'Mr Willingham has been taken into custody?' asked Rebecca. She was curious, now that things had been resolved so happily between them, to know Mr Willingham's fate.

'Yes. He will be charged with his crimes, and Cyril Dunn will testify against him. Mr Willingham will not be troubling us again.'

Rebecca gave a shiver. 'He came so close to killing you.'

Joshua held her tight. 'But he didn't. It's over now, and the future is before us. And talking of the future,' he said, turning towards her, 'I think we should be planning our wedding. When shall it be?'

'In the summer, I think,' said Rebecca.

The clock chimed the hour.

'Goodness. I had no idea how late it was. I had forgotten all about Louisa!' exclaimed Rebecca. She stood up. 'She will be wondering where I am.'

Joshua stood up, too. 'She has most probably guessed.'

'You're right. But we must go and find her anyway. I want to tell her the news.'

'She'll be delighted,' said Joshua. Adding, 'And so will Mrs Camberwell.'

Rebecca looked at him in surprise.

'She has spent the last few weeks telling me what a wonderful wife you will make,' he laughed.

Rebecca smiled, then gave a contented sigh. 'It's lovely to know that our betrothal will bring so much pleasure to so many people.'

'Not least to ourselves.' He took her into his arms and kissed her.

'If you don't stop kissing me like that, I will not be able to wait for a summer wedding,' she teased him as she at last emerged.

He pulled her into his arms and kissed her again. 'A good thing too. Hang the gossips. If they want to remark on the speed of our wedding then let them - I have always thought spring weddings were the best.'

'Perhaps they are at that!'

Then arm in arm they went to find Louisa and tell her the happy news.

Author's Note

Readers might like to know that the Frost Fair mentioned in this book actually took place in 1814. The climate then was colder than it is now and the river flowed more slowly for a variety of reasons, including the fact that the old London Bridge had narrow arches which impeded the flow of water. The entertainments enjoyed by Rebecca and Joshua in this book were enjoyed by revellers at the time. It was, however, the last Frost Fair.

Printed in Great Britain
by Amazon.co.uk, Ltd.,
Marston Gate.